EYRBYGGJA SAGA

TRANSLATED WITH AN INTRODUCTION
AND NOTES BY
HERMANN PÁLSSON
AND
PAUL EDWARDS

PENGUIN BOOKS

PENGUIN BOOKS

Published by the Penguin Group
Penguin Books Ltd, 80 Strand, London WC2R 0RL, England
Penguin Putnam Inc., 375 Hudson Street, New York, New York 10014, USA
Penguin Books Australia Ltd, 250 Camberwell Road, Camberwell, Victoria 3124, Australia
Penguin Books Canada Ltd, 10 Alcorn Avenue, Toronto, Ontario, Canada M4V 3B2
Penguin Books India (P) Ltd, 11 Community Centre, Panchsheel Park, New Delhi – 110 017, India
Penguin Books (NZ) Ltd, Cnr Rosedale and Airborne Roads, Albany, Auckland, New Zealand
Penguin Books (South Africa) (Pty) Ltd, 24 Sturdee Avenue, Rosebank 2196, South Africa

Penguin Books Ltd, Registered Offices: 80 Strand, London WC2R 0RL, England

www.penguin.com

First published by Southside (Publishers) Ltd 1972
Published, with extensive revisions, in Penguin Books 1989

14

Translation, introduction and notes
copyright © Hermann Pálsson and Paul Edwards, 1972, 1989
All rights reserved

Printed in the United States of America
Filmset in Palatino (Linotron 202)

PENGUIN CLASSICS

EYRBYGGJA SAGA

HERMANN PÁLSSON studied Icelandic at the University of Iceland and Celtic at University College, Dublin. He was formerly Professor of Icelandic at the University of Edinburgh, where he taught from 1950 to 1988. He is the General Editor of the New Saga Library and the author of many books on the history and literature of medieval Iceland; his more recent publications include *Legendary Fiction in Medieval Iceland* (with Paul Edwards), *Art and Ethics in Hrafnkel's Saga* and *Vikings in Russia* (with Paul Edwards). Hermann Pálsson has also translated *Hrafnkel's Saga*, and collaborated with Magnus Magnusson in translating *Laxdæla Saga*, *The Vinland Sagas*, *King Harald's Saga* and *Njal's Saga* for the Penguin Classics.

PAUL EDWARDS read English at Durham University, Celtic and Icelandic at Cambridge, and then worked in West Africa for nine years. He was Professor of English and African Literature at Edinburgh University until his death in May 1992. In addition to books on Icelandic studies with Hermann Pálsson, he published books and articles on African history, and on English and African literature.

HERMANN PÁLSSON and PAUL EDWARDS also translated *Egil's Saga*, *Orkneyinga Saga* and *Seven Viking Romances* for Penguin Classics. Their translations of *Knytlinga Saga*, *The Book of Settlements*, *Magnus' Saga*, *Hrolf Gautreksson* and *Göngu-Hrolf's Saga* have been published elsewhere.

CONTENTS

viii   *Contents*

INTRODUCTION

Writing in 1813, Sir Walter Scott says that 'of all the various records of Icelandic history and literature, there is none more interesting than *Eyrbyggja Saga*'.[1] It is not surprising that a novelist as fascinated by the past as Scott should so respond to the world of *Eyrbyggja Saga*, which indeed is in many respects akin to that of the romantic imagination. There are antiquarian elements, such as the detailed (though largely invented) description of the temple at Thor's Ness and of the duties of a pagan priesthood; there are gothic elements, such as the eerie hauntings at Frodriver and the unquiet graves of the malevolent dead; and along with these there are violent encounters with vikings and berserks and a pervasive heroic spirit. But the author of the *Waverley Novels* must have been still more powerfully fascinated by the elaborate structure of a narrative in which the lives of many remarkable and varied individuals are set against a background of actual historical events to produce an imaginative view of history. For it must be stressed at once that although the saga often seems to be recording history, its true spirit is imaginative and interpretative, a thirteenth-century view of the past. As Magnus Magnusson remarks,

These Sagas of Icelanders . . . were written in the vernacular, in prose, and can best be described as historical novels – the first novels to be written in Europe. They were not, strictly speaking, histories; they were imaginative works of art created around an historical framework and using many different sources: written records and genealogies, traditional oral stories, earlier sagas, fragments of remembered verses uttered on special occasions. Their purpose was to

---

1. Sir Walter Scott, 'Abstract of the Eyrbyggja-Saga', in M. Mallet, (ed.), *Illustrations of Northern Antiquities* (Edinburgh, 1814). Our reference is to the edition of 1847, p. 517.

entertain and edify their audience, like the great novels of the nineteenth century.[2]

It is interesting that Scott's appraisal of *Eyrbyggja Saga* as a proto-historical novel was written at Abbotsford in 1813, one year before the publication of the first of the *Waverley Novels*. Later Scottish novelists have also borrowed from *Eyrbyggja Saga*: R. L. Stevenson in his tale *The Waif Woman*, and Eric Linklater in his enjoyable pastiche-saga, *The Men of Ness*.

On the surface, *Eyrbyggja Saga* reads like an historical record, tracing the lives of several generations from the late ninth century to the early eleventh. The narrative opens with the pagan anarchy of the Viking Age, but moves rapidly to an account of the settlement of Iceland and the beginnings of an organized society. A period of internal strain and violence, as the laws are hammered out on the lives of spirited and in-flexible individuals, closes with the arrival of Christianity and the gradual establishment of the ordered civilization of medieval Iceland early in the eleventh century. Later we shall examine the artistic pattern of the saga in some detail and shall have more to say about its historical framework: at this point, however, we might generalize and say that *Eyrbyggja Saga* describes a community progressing from lawlessness to collective responsibility. But by the time the saga was written in the thirteenth century, Icelandic society was both politically and economically in decline, and so it could be seen as essentially nostalgic, reflecting pride in the past rather than in the author's own times, though that nostalgia shows no trace of sentimentality, and the past is seen as in many respects harsh and uncompromising.

The precise date and provenance of *Eyrbyggja Saga* are matters for speculation; and, as with the other Sagas of Ice-landers, its author is unknown. All the same, it seems likely that it was composed not long after the middle of the thirteenth century, and quite probably at Helgafell, the focal place of the

2. Magnus Magnusson, *Iceland Saga* (London, 1987), p. 21.

story. It is tempting to speculate that it may have been written in the Augustinian house founded at Helgafell in 1184 and an important intellectual centre and scriptorium right through to the end of the medieval period. A number of manuscripts still extant were written by priests who were either inmates of the house, or had been trained there. Two of the heads of the house were direct descendants of Snorri the Priest, the main figure of *Eyrbyggja Saga*: these were Thorfinn Thorgeirsson (1188–1216) and Ketil Hermundarson (1217–30). It was at Helgafell, too, that Ari Thorgilsson the Learned, Iceland's first vernacular historian, was born. There was a considerable library there of nearly 120 books around the year 1186, and towards the end of the fourteenth century about 120 books in Latin and 35 in Icelandic. It has been suggested that *Laxdæla Saga* and *Eyrbyggja Saga* were composed at about the same time by two members of the house at Helgafell, and that they used each other's work, for each saga shows knowledge of the other. This would explain why Helgafell becomes the focal place of *Laxdæla Saga* precisely at the point where it ceases to be that of *Eyrbyggja Saga*.[3]

The structure of the saga is so complicated that many readers have compared it unfavourably with *Njal's Saga*, *Gisli's Saga*, or *Grettir's Saga*, in which the hero's life is so central to the narrative that it provides a clearly defined structural core, no matter what the surrounding complexities may be.[4] Once *Eyrbyggja Saga* is read in its own terms, rather than in terms of the organization of other, deceptively similar sagas, distinct patterns begin to emerge. These patterns display an inter-relation of families and individuals in two dimensions. First

---

3. Late in *Eyrbyggja Saga* (Chapter 56) we are told that 'in the spring Snorri exchanged farms with Gudrun, Osvif's-daughter . . .'. *Laxdæla Saga* (Chapter 56) records Gudrun's move to Helgafell.

4. These sagas explore a central eponymous tragic figure, but *Eyrbyggja Saga* might be said to differ from them in the way that Shakespeare's tragedies differ from the great tetralogy of history plays, in which figures such as Richard II or Hotspur play potentially tragic roles, but the focus of the plays is on the land itself.

there is the linear movement from the ninth to the eleventh century, from the first settlers to their great-grandchildren. Then there are all the complex social relationships between these people living in a small community, bound by duties often arising out of marriage ties, or out of enmities caused by the grabbing of land or the killing of a kinsman. The pattern could best be illustrated by guiding the reader initially through the events of the saga and pointing out the landmarks. The saga might be broken down into eight sections, as follows:

1. *Prologue* (Chapters 1–8). This describes the rise of Harald Fine-Hair, King of Norway, and the pressure placed upon certain powerful and rebellious chieftains and landowners who are unwilling to accept Harald's rule. Under these pressures a number of them leave Norway, some going to the newly discovered, uninhabited land called Iceland. Two of these in particular are described, Thorolf Mostur-Beard and Bjorn the Easterner. Thorolf is a priest of Thor, and establishes strict rules of conduct:

Thorolf gave the name Thor's Ness to the region between Vigra Fjord and Hofsvag. On this headland is a mountain held so sacred by Thorolf that no one was allowed even to look at it without first having washed himself, and no living creature on this mountain, neither man nor beast, was to be harmed until it left of its own accord. Thorolf called this mountain Helga Fell and believed that he and his kinsmen would go into it when they died.

Thorolf used to hold all his courts on the point of the headland where Thor had come ashore, and that was where he started the district assembly. This place was so holy that he would let no one desecrate it, either with bloodshed or with excrement; and for a privy they used a special rock in the sea which they called Dritsker [literally, 'Dirt Skerry'].[5]

Bjorn's respect for the old gods is also made clear, and at this point in the narrative there is no reason to expect anything but

5. See pp. 29–30.

friendship between the descendants of these two founder-fathers, Thorolf and Bjorn the Easterner.

2. *Quarrels between Thorsnessings and Kjalleklings* (Chapter 9–28). In the next generation, however, trouble begins between the people of Thor's Ness, who are descendants of Thorolf, called the Thorsnessings, and the sons of Kjallak, Bjorn the Easterner's grandchildren. Both families have become very powerful, and family pride leads to conflict. Quarrels begin over what might appear at first sight a trivial and rather comical matter, the refusal of the Kjalleklings to go out to Dritsker to ease themselves. But the descendants of Thorolf take their attempted desecration of the holy place very seriously indeed, and tensions build up, in spite of efforts at peacemaking, to a series of clashes. In due course a battle is fought between the followers of Thorarin the Black (related by marriage to the Kjalleklings) and Thorbjorn the Stout (related by marriage to Snorri the Priest, descendant of Thorolf Mostur-Beard). Once again the basis of the quarrel, the alleged theft of some horses, hardly seems to justify the bitterness of feelings and the killings that follow. But the very triviality of the surface causes of conflict only serves to emphasize the undercurrents of unreasoning pride and smouldering neurotic violence. This particular sequence of quarrels slowly resolves itself, mainly as a result of the skilful manœuvrings of Snorri, who ends up giving advice and aid over two troublesome berserks belonging to Styr, one of the leading men of the Kjallekling clan. The berserks are killed; Snorri marries Styr's-daughter; Thorarin the Black goes overseas and is, we are told, 'now out of the story'. This, however, is only a lull, and a new set of tensions has already begun to develop, to explode into violence in the next part of the story. Indeed, the enmity between the descendants of Thorolf and those of Bjorn rears up from under the surface of many a subsequent conflict.

3. *The Conflict between Snorri and Arnkel* (Chapters 29–38).

Arnkel is the virtuous but strong-minded son of a malicious viking settler, Thorolf Twist-Foot, and, like Snorri, a great man and a temple priest. Since he and Snorri are the two greatest men in the district, people with lawsuits naturally come to them for guidance and support. The seeds of conflict have earlier been sown over Snorri's killing of a man called Vigfus. With the support of the Kjalleklings, Arnkel had taken up the case against Snorri on behalf of Vigfus's kin. Now once again it seems that pride and honour will not allow two cocks to crow in the same district. Arnkel had inherited the fighting qualities of his viking father, without his malice, for he also has the generosity of spirit shown by his grandmother Geirrid:

She built a hall right across the main road, and every traveller was expected to pass through it. In the hall stood a table always laden with food, which all were welcome to share, and for this people thought her the finest of women.[6]

It is inevitable that a man as great-hearted and as firm-minded as Arnkel should come into conflict with the cunning and ambivalent Snorri, about whom we shall have more to say in due course. In his purity of motive and his strength of purpose, Arnkel is what Snorri is to become in the later stages of the narrative. Tensions culminate in the heroic last stand of Arnkel, alone against Snorri and his blood-brothers, the trouble-making Thorbrandssons. Arnkel is killed, but his death is lamented as a great loss, and as an indication of what is wrong with this society:

Arnkel was mourned by everyone, for of all men in pagan times he was the most gifted. He was remarkably shrewd in judgement, good-tempered, kind-hearted, brave, honest, and moderate. He came out on top in every lawsuit, no matter with whom he had to deal, which explains why people were so envious of him, as is shown by the way he met his death.[7]

6. See p. 33.
7. See pp. 100–102.

Since Arnkel leaves no male heir to take legal action over his killing, Snorri gets off very lightly. That the death of a man as outstanding as Arnkel should be so neglected in law is seen as a social disgrace, and the author makes the point that in consequence the law was changed. So we are made aware of the growing social responsibility underlying all the violence and pride. However, another sequence has been completed, Arnkel is dead, and Snorri's power continues to increase.

4. *Snorri and the Thorbrandssons versus Bjorn and the Thorlakssons* (Chapters 39–48). Yet another set of enmities has been developing during the previous sequence of events. Snorri's blood-brothers, the Thorbrandssons, who aided him in the attack on Arnkel, are now in conflict with a group called the Thorlakssons, who are living at Eyr. Snorri is also at odds with a man from Breidavik, Bjorn Asbrandsson, who has been having an affair with Snorri's married sister Thurid. It is generally known, though apparently not talked about, that Thurid's son, Kjartan, is the child of Bjorn, not of her husband Thorodd. In his disgrace, Thorodd has appealed to Snorri for help, so that now these new conflicting groups are ranged against one another. The surface causes of tension are as usual quite trivial – a blow with a hot porridge-ladle, a piece of turf thrown in a game – but the cuckolding of Thorodd sharpens the tension; Snorri secretly sends a slave on a mission to kill one of the men of Breidavik; Bjorn and his brother catch and kill the slave; and once more violence breaks out. There are two major battles, Alfta Fjord and Vigra Fjord, and the strain which is being put on society is clearly marked by the dilemma of Styr, who is not only a Kjallekling, related to the Thorlakssons, and so tied by blood to Snorri's enemies, but is also Snorri's father-in-law, and indebted to him for help given against the troublesome berserks. At the Battle of Alfta Fjord, Styr is fighting on the side of his kinsmen the Thorlakssons against Snorri. But when Snorri's twelve-year-old son (and so Styr's

own grandson) is wounded, Snorri exaggerates, telling Styr
that the boy is dying:

[Styr] claimed the first victim when he killed a man on Snorri's, his own
son-in-law's, side. Snorri saw it happen. 'Is this how you avenge your
grandson Thorodd,' he asked, 'when he's dying of the wound
Steinthor gave him? You're no better than a traitor!'
　'I can soon make it up to you,' said Styr, and with that he changed
sides. He joined Snorri with all his followers, and the next man he
killed was one of Steinthor's.[8]

Yet again the author draws attention to the enormous pressure
these conflicts are placing on society. In due course, peace
terms are agreed – 'The killings by Styr, one on each side,
cancelled each other out,' we are told – but the matter of
Bjorn's affair with Thurid is still to be settled. In a brilliant
dramatic episode Snorri sets out to kill Bjorn, dressed in
the blue cloak characteristically worn by the killer in the
sagas:

Bjorn watched the riders coming down from the moor into the
meadow and recognized them at once, with Snorri the Priest in the
lead wearing a blue cloak. Then Bjorn made a daring move. He picked
up the knife and walked straight towards them. When he got to
Snorri, he took hold of his cloak-sleeve with one hand and pointed the
knife right at Snorri's chest with the other, ready to drive it home
directly. He greeted them, and Snorri returned his greeting, but
Mar lost his nerve when he saw how easily Bjorn could stab
Snorri if anyone tried to rush him. Bjorn walked them on their
way and asked the news, without relaxing the firm grip he had on
Snorri.[9]

Still, Snorri gets his way without violence, for he manages to
persuade Bjorn to leave Iceland; and so Bjorn is to all intents
'out of the story', though he is to reappear right at the end of
the narrative in a brief, mysterious episode set in an unknown
land across the sea.

8. See pp. 117–18.
9. See p. 126.

5. *Christianity and the Ghosts* (Chapters 49–55). Christianity now reaches Iceland, and the mode of the story undergoes certain changes. It is Snorri, lawyer, warrior, killer, priest of Thor, who now does more than anyone to persuade the Icelanders to embrace Christianity. There is an entertaining episode in which two women briefly take a central place in the story: Thorgunna, a rich, middle-aged immigrant from the Hebrides, and Thurid, Bjorn's mistress and Snorri's sister, who has taken a liking to Thorgunna's fine clothes and splendid bed-furnishings. But the tone of the episode grows increasingly ominous as Thorgunna's death introduces a series of hauntings which have been hinted at earlier in the death and burial of Arnkel's evil-hearted viking father, Thorolf Twist-Foot. Now the ghosts of old Iceland take the centre of the stage, confronting the new religion. There are a number of echoes from the pagan past; Thorodd and the drowned men who visit the Christmas home-fires of Frodriver will remind the reader of the fires and feasting of the drowned Thorstein the Cod-Biter and his men inside the holy mountain of Helga Fell early on in the story.[10] But Snorri gives advice, and the ghosts are banished by a significant combination, the old law and the new religion. First of all the ghosts are summoned to a 'door-court' and leave reluctantly when they are found legally guilty of trespassing. Then prayers are said, holy water is sprinkled, and the land is disinfected of its unholy past. But there is another element of the pagan past which has to be exorcized along with the ghosts, and that is the world of the vikings, the violence and crime that have bedevilled society's struggle towards order. This is the subject of the next episode.

6. *Snorri against Ospak and the Vikings* (Chapters 56–62). A viking called Ospak begins to raid and kill, grabbing loot wherever he and his men can lay hands on it, and causing havoc in the farming community, where people are neither

10. See p. 38.

powerful enough nor violent enough to defend themselves effectively against this arbitrary onslaught from the past. At first Snorri, characteristically, does little but wait – 'he let people talk' – but the crafty lawyer and killer has been undergoing a slow change towards social responsibility. He now acts on behalf of society against lawlessness, leading the farmers in battle against the outlaws, killing their leaders and coming to terms with the rest.

7. *Echoes from the Past* (Chapters 63–4). The scene is set for the dying cadences of the narrative, remembrances of the past as it fades with a distant rumble of the ancient thunder. The blackened, uncorrupted corpse of the villainous Thorolf Twist-Foot rises from his grave, and is the last of the ghosts to be laid, taking with him Thorodd Thorbrandsson, another old troublemaker, a survivor of the Battle of Vigra Fjord and one of Snorri's companions in the killing of Thorolf Twist-Foot's son, the noble Arnkel. As Thorolf's spirit, in the form of a demonic bull, takes the life of the farmer Thorodd and vanishes for ever into a swamp, remote echoes of jealousy and violence fade from the narrative. An entirely new figure, Gudleif, meets a mysterious old chieftain in a strange, undefined country where his ship has been driven in a storm, and it turns out that this is none other than Bjorn, the lover of Thurid and father of Kjartan. But he will not declare his name openly, insists that no one must ever visit him – indeed they cannot, for the land where he lives is never precisely located – and vanishes from the naturalistic part of the narrative just as Thorolf's ghost has vanished from the supernaturalistic.

8. *Epilogue* (Chapter 65). The narrative from which Snorri has emerged as the principal figure, illustrative of the best and the worst, growing in stature throughout the story, ends with the listing of his kin, his sons, his daughters, their children, and the farms on which they live. But the bones of the dead no longer rise to create trouble amongst the living:

Snorri the Priest died at Tongue in Sælingsdale a year after the killing of King Olaf the Saint, and was buried at the church he himself had built. When the graveyard there was changed, his bones were removed to the site of the present church. Gudny, Bodvar's-daughter, was present, the mother of the Sturlusons, Snorri, Thord, and Sighvat, and she said that Snorri the Priest's bones were those of a man of average height, not very tall. She also said that the bones of Snorri's uncle, Bork the Stout, had been dug up and that they were exceptionally big. The bones of old Thordis, Sur's-daughter, were dug up too, and Gudny said they were those of a small woman, and black as if they had been singed. All these bones were buried again at the place where the church now stands.[11]

Snorri has been the outstanding, most ambivalent figure in the story. His very name means 'turbulent' and is given him in place of his original name Thorgrim because he is 'a very difficult child'. He is born in violence, for only a few days before his birth, his father is killed in the course of a vendetta by Gisli, the hero of *Gisli's Saga*. Snorri's mother Thordis marries his father's brother, Bork, and as in the story of Hamlet there are further tensions here. Snorri takes sides with his mother against his stepfather, and indeed husband and wife are locked in conflict, for Gisli, the killer of Snorri's father, is also the brother of Thordis, his mother, and she, like her son, is torn between conflicting duties. Snorri exhibits contradictory impulses throughout his life. He can fight bravely and honourably, but he is also capable of sending a criminal to kill his enemy by stealth. He is a peacemaker one moment, a man of blood the next. The narrator regularly speculates on Snorri's motives: at one point, when Snorri is making peace, the narrator adds that people believe Snorri only did so because he saw distant reinforcements on the way to join his opponents. The Thorbrandssons send a slave, Egil, to kill Bjorn and his brother, but the narrator adds that 'some people think Snorri the Priest was behind the plot.' Snorri is a pagan priest, yet as we have said, he does more than anyone to persuade the Icelanders to embrace Christianity. Though he emerges from

11. See pp. 165–6.

the tale as a distinct personality, little about that personality is unambiguous, as the narrator suggests in this description of Snorri:

Snorri was of medium height and rather slight build, a handsome, regular-featured man with a fair complexion, flaxen hair, and a reddish beard. He was usually even-tempered, and it was hard to tell whether he was pleased or not. He was a very shrewd man with unusual foresight, a long memory, and a taste for vengeance. To his friends he gave good counsel, but his enemies learned to fear the advice he gave. As Snorri was now in charge of the temple he was called Snorri the Priest. He became a man of great power, and some people envied him bitterly, . . .[12]

In fact, he is the very epitome both of the stresses within early Icelandic society, and of its growth from lawlessness to order and discipline. To Walter Scott, Snorri was the most fascinating figure in the most fascinating of sagas:

That such a character, partaking more of the jurisconsult or statesman than of the warrior, should have risen so high in such an early period, argues the preference which the Icelanders already assigned to mental superiority over the rude attributes of strength and courage, and furnishes another proof of the early civilization of this extraordinary commonwealth.[13]

Eyrbyggja Saga, of course, was not created in a vacuum, and it belongs to the main stream of medieval Icelandic literary tradition. As we have said, it was probably written shortly after the middle of the thirteenth century at a time when many sagas had already been composed. The author uses a number of written sources: several chapters derive from the *Book of Settlements* (*Landnámabók*), probably the version, now lost, of Styrmir Kárason (d. 1245). The earliest extant version of the *Book of Settlements*, that of Sturla Thordarson (1214–84) in turn added material taken from *Eyrbyggja Saga*, and so one text

12. See pp. 44–5.
13. Scott, 'Abstract of the Eyrbyggja-Saga' in Mallet, op. cit., pp. 539–40.

cross-fertilizes another. Several sagas are referred to in *Eyrbyggja Saga*: Chapter 24 gives a summary of part of *Eirik's Saga*;[14] the killing of Snorri's father and other elements in the story refer to *Gisli's Saga*; and the author also uses *Laxdæla Saga*[15] and *Heidarviga Saga*. Thus, while *Eyrbyggja Saga* draws upon historical records, it also belongs to the great tradition of story-telling, and must be seen as fictionalized history. It would be a mistake to think of it as a factual historical account, and elements of authorial fancy and design can easily be demonstrated. At the same time, it is useful to see the framework of chronology upon which the events of the tale are founded, as they are recorded in the *Icelandic Annals*:

874	Ingolf Arnarson goes to Iceland.[16]
918	Thorolf Mostur-Beard dies.
938	Thorgrim the Priest (father of Snorri) is born.
952	Thorbjorn Sur (father of Thordis, Snorri's mother) comes to Iceland.
963	Thorgrim the Priest is killed, Snorri is born.
986	Eirik the Red colonizes Greenland.
1000	Christianity is adopted by law.
1008	Styr (Snorri's father-in-law) is killed.
1031	Snorri dies.
1112	Thurid Snorri's-daughter dies aged 88.

Well-informed people like old Thurid would offer the twelfth-century Icelandic historian a long unbroken link with the past; and she was in fact one of the informants of Ari the Learned (1068–1148), author of the *Book of Icelanders* (*Íslendingabók*) and co-author of the first version of the *Book of Settlements*. As already mentioned, a later version of the latter was probably used by the author of *Eyrbyggja Saga*, and his imaginative and inventive powers would be able to play with confidence upon

14. In *The Vinland Sagas*, (Penguin Classics, 1963).
15. *Laxdæla Saga* (Penguin Classics, 1969).
16. Compare account in *Eyrbyggja Saga* (Chapter 3, p. 27) of Thorolf Mostur-Beard's emigration: 'This was ten years after Ingolf Arnarson had sailed off to settle in Iceland.'

such firmly based history and chronology as this and the *Icelandic Annals*.

As we have already observed, however, the author takes pleasure in the antiquarian as well as in the more specifically historical. His attempt to describe the temple of Thor (Chapter 4) illustrates the fascination which the past held for the thirteenth-century Icelander much better than it records pagan customs, and indeed when we come to the great hauntings at Frodriver it is apparent that the author's gothic imagination is excitedly at work. Again and again, however, we hear such phrases as 'it was the law in those days', or 'as people did in those days', or 'according to ancient custom'. The author is interested in omens, in the speaking head on Geirvör, in the black cloud that rains blood before the death of Thorgunna, and he regularly organizes scenes in such a way that they have a quality of inevitability which is splendid drama, but hardly acceptable as history. But he is interested, too, in the actual physical landmarks of the past: of the berserks' wall he says, 'you can still see traces of it'; of Thor's Stone, 'you can still see the blood on the stone'; of the wall built behind Thorolf Twist-Foot's grave, 'you can still see traces of the wall there'. The geography is another accurately recorded feature, and a strong contributory factor to the impression of realism is the description of everyday activities, of farming and fishing, tools, techniques, and the organization of domestic routines. Though in some respects the world of *Eyrbyggja Saga* was remote from that of its author – the vikings, the old gods, the witchcraft, for example – in others it was still close, for the methods of farming, the kind of homes people lived in, the assemblies they attended, were still much the same. But perhaps more than anything else, the delineation of character persuades us of the reality of this mixed world of the marvellous and the commonplace, the historically accurate and the artfully designed.

We have seen already in the case of Snorri how the author is interested in complexities of character and the relationship of character to background. The virtuous Arnkel, Snorri's opponent in a major section of the narrative, is more simply drawn, but even here one recognizes the author's sense, not only of what men inherit from their parents, but also of what they reject. Arnkel displays his father's best qualities as a fighting man, but reacts against his malicious trouble-making, inheriting the generosity and openness of his grandmother Geirrid, who built her hall across the road and had tables ready-laden with food for hungry travellers. Thorolf Twist-Foot himself can be seen as reacting against the best qualities of his mother:

Thorolf thought the land which his mother had taken not nearly extensive enough, so he challenged Ulfar the Champion to single combat for the land he owned, Ulfar being old and childless.[17]

And the narrator tells us that Thorolf 'was a very hard man'. So tensions within the family are being established which will not only become crucial to the development of the plot, but also lead to acute observations on human conduct. Thorolf tries to persuade Arnkel to take action against Snorri over a stretch of woodland. Arnkel refuses (even though he wishes to take action and indeed does so after his father's death), simply because his father urges it, and he must react against him. Thorolf goes off home in a rage, and appropriately it seems to be of rage that he dies:

Thorolf went back home in a rage for he could see how difficult it was going to be for him to get what he wanted. It was evening when he reached home and he sat down on the high-seat without uttering a word to anybody. He ate nothing all evening and stayed in his seat when the rest of the household went to bed. In the morning, when they got up, Thorolf was still sitting there, dead.[18]

The author's pleasure in less grim aspects of character can be seen in the relationship between Thurid and Thorgunna, with Thurid unable to keep her eyes, and ultimately her hands, off

17. See p. 33.   18. See p. 92.

Thorgunna's fine and fashionable clothes and her magnificent bedding. Thorgunna herself, by no means a major figure in the story, is splendidly presented:

Thorgunna spent every day weaving, unless there was haymaking to do, and when the weather was good, she used to work at drying the hay in the home meadow. She had a special rake made for her which she would let no one else touch. Thorgunna was a massive woman, tall, broad-built, and getting very stout. She had dark eyebrows and narrow eyes, and beautiful chestnut hair. Her manner was always very proper, and she used to go to Mass every morning before starting work, but she was hard to get on with and wasted little time on conversation. People thought she must be in her fifties, though she was a woman who still had a lot of life in her.[19]

The last sentence particularly takes on a sharper significance when we learn that Thorgunna has taken a fancy to someone:

Kjartan the farmer's son was the only one there Thorgunna took to, and she liked him a lot, but he kept his distance, which she found extremely irritating. Kjartan was thirteen or fourteen at the time, a big lad, and very manly.[20]

This domineering, irascible, ageing, still sexually active woman with an eye for a likely lad is sketched here in a few precise strokes. It seems appropriate that when the dead Thorgunna is being taken some distance for burial, her corpse should rise up and cook a meal for the coffin-bearers, stark naked, and as domineering as ever.

19. See p. 130.   20. See p. 130.

NOTE ON THE TRANSLATION

The present translation is based on Einar Olafur Sveinsson's standard edition in *Íslenzk Fornrit*, vol. 4 (Reykjavík, 1935). Earlier translations and editions are listed in the Bibliographical Notes on pp. 174–7.

We first translated this saga for Southside (Publishers) Ltd in 1972, but in the present version we have made extensive revisions.

Edinburgh, 1988   HERMANN PÁLSSON
                                                 PAUL EDWARDS

LIST OF CHARACTERS

1. THE THORSNESSINGS

THOROLF MOSTUR-BEARD	*a settler from Norway*
THORSTEIN COD-BITER	*founder of Helgafell, his son*
BORK THE STOUT	*sons of Thorstein the Cod-Biter*
THORGRIM THE PRIEST	
THORDIS	*wife of Thorgrim, and later married to Bork*
SNORRI THE PRIEST	*son of Thorgrim and Thordis*
THURID	*daughter of Bork and Thordis, second wife of Thorbjorn the Stout of Frodriver*

2. THE KJALLEKLINGS

BJORN THE EASTERNER	*of Bjorn's Haven, a settler from Norway*
KJALLAK THE OLD	*his children*
HELGA, wife of Asgeir of Eyr	
THORGRIM THE PRIEST	*of Bjorn's Haven, son of Kjallak the Old*
VERMUND THE SLENDER, of Bjorn's Haven	*sons of Thorgrim*
KILLER-STYR, of Hraun	
VIGFUS OF DRAPUHLID	*a distant relative*

3. ARNKEL'S FAMILY

GEIRROD	*a settler*
GEIRRID	*of Borgardale, his sister*
THOROLF TWIST-FOOT	*of Hvamm, her son*
ARNKEL THE PRIEST, of Bolstad GEIRRID OF MAVAHLID	} *children of Thorolf Twist-Foot*
THORGERD	*their niece,* *wife of Vigfus of Drapuhlid*
THORARIN THE BLACK GUDNY, wife of Killer-Styr	} *children of Geirrid of Mavahlid*

4. THE MEN OF EYR

VESTAR	*a settler*
ASGEIR	*his son*
THORLAK	*son of Asgeir*
STEINTHOR THORMOD BERGTHOR THORD BLIG	} *sons of Thorlak*

5. THE MEN OF BREIDAVIK

ASBRAND OF KAMB

BJORN the Breidavik-
Champion
ARINBJORN THE STRONG   *his children*
THURID, first wife of
Thorbjorn the Stout of
Frodriver

GUNNLAUG   *son of Thorbjorn and Thurid*

6. THE MEN OF ALFTAFJORD

FINNGEIR   *a settler*

THORFINN   *his son*

THORBRAND   *son of Thorfinn*

THORLEIF KIMBI
SNORRI
THORODD   *sons of Thorbrand*
THORFINN
THORMOD

FREYSTEIN BOFI   *foster-son of Thorbrand*

EYRBYGGJA SAGA

1. KETIL FLAT-NOSE

There was a great chieftain in Norway called Ketil Flat-Nose, the son of Bjorn Buna, son of Grim, one of the leading men in Sogn. Ketil was married to Yngvild, the daughter of Ketil Wether, a chieftain in Romerike. Their sons were Bjorn and Helgi, and their daughters Aud the Deep-Minded, Thorunn Hyrna, and Jorunn Wisdom-Slope.[1] Bjorn Ketilsson was brought up east in Jamtaland by Earl Kjallak, a wise man and very highly thought of. Earl Kjallak had a son called Bjorn, too, as well as a daughter, Gjaflaug.

Just about that time King Harald Fine-Hair was forcing his way to power in Norway.[2] During the campaign many men of high standing abandoned their estates in Norway, some emigrating east across the Kjolen Mountains, some west over the North Sea. Others used to winter in the Hebrides or in Orkney, then spend the summers raiding in Harald's kingdom, causing plenty of damage. When the farmers complained about it to the King and asked him to get rid of these trouble-makers, he planned an expedition west over the sea with Ketil Flat-Nose in command. Ketil tried to talk his way out of it, but the King said Ketil would have to go; and once he realized that the King was determined to have his own way, Ketil got ready for the voyage, taking his wife along and those children of his who happened to be with him.

After having landed in the west, Ketil fought a number of battles, and won them all. He conquered and took charge of the Hebrides, making peace and alliances with all the leading men there in the west. After that, Ketil sent the troops back to

1. For Ketil Flat-Nose and his children, see also *The Book of Settlements*, Chapter 13, and *Laxdæla Saga* (Penguin Classics, 1969), pp. 47–67.
2. The events described in Chapters 1–2 are evidently supposed to have occurred c.865–75. According to the *Icelandic Annals*, King Harald ruled for 70 years and died in 931.

Norway. When they came to King Harald, they told him how Ketil Flat-Nose had taken over in the Hebrides, but without doing much to bring the islands under King Harald's rule. Once the King heard this, he confiscated all Ketil's estates in Norway.

Ketil Flat-Nose arranged the marriage of his daughter Aud to Olaf the White, the greatest warrior-king at that time in the British Isles. Olaf was the son of Ingjald Helgason and Thora, daughter of Sigurd Snake-in-the-Eye, son of Ragnar Hairy-Breeks. His other daughter, Thorunn Hyrna, Ketil married to Helgi the Lean, son of Eyvind the Easterner and of Rafarta, daughter of King Kjarval of Ireland.

❧

2. BJORN IS OUTLAWED

Bjorn, son of Ketil Flat-Nose stayed on in Jamtaland until Earl Kjallak died, then married the Earl's daughter Gjaflaug, and after that travelled west across the Kjolen Mountains, first to Trondheim, then south from there to his father's estates, where he took command and threw out the stewards King Harald had put in charge.

King Harald was in Oslo Fjord when he heard of this, and wasted no time before setting out across the mountains towards Trondheim. When he arrived, Harald called people together from eight provinces and formally declared Bjorn Ketilsson an outlaw in Norway, which meant that anyone could lawfully kill him, if they could catch him. The King sent Hauk Long-Breeks and some other warriors to execute Bjorn if he could be found. But when these men came south to Stad, Bjorn's friends got wind of their mission and warned him, so Bjorn jumped into a small ship he owned and sailed off with his household and goods. Since it was the worst time of winter, he decided not to risk the open sea but kept south along the coast instead, sailing on till he reached Mostur Island off South Hordaland. A man there called Hrolf, son of Ornolf the Fish-Driver, gave him a friendly welcome, so Bjorn stayed on in hiding there for the rest of the winter. The King's agents went back north as soon as they had settled matters about Bjorn's estates and put people in charge of them.

❦

3. THOROLF MOSTUR-BEARD

Besides running a good farm, this Hrolf was a chieftain of considerable standing. He was a close friend of Thor, and had charge of Thor's temple there on the island, so people called him Thorolf. A tall, powerful man, Thorolf was very handsome and his long beard got him the nickname Mostur-Beard. He was respected above all other men on the island.

In the spring Thorolf gave Bjorn a fine longship with a good fighting crew, and sent his son Hallstein voyaging with him. They sailed west across the North Sea and joined up with Bjorn's kinsmen.

When King Harald heard that Thorolf Mostur-Beard had been sheltering his outlaw Bjorn Ketilsson, he sent messengers dismissing Thorolf from his estates, with the warning that unless he gave himself up and placed himself in the King's hands, he would be outlawed like his friend Bjorn. This was ten years after Ingolf Arnarson had sailed off to settle in Iceland, a voyage that was on everyone's lips. People coming back from Iceland had nothing but good to say of it.[1]

1. According to Ari Thorgilsson's *Book of Icelanders* (written *c*. 1125), Ingolf Arnarson, the first Norwegian to make his permanent home in Iceland, went there in 870, 'about the time when St Edmund of East Anglia was martyred by the Vikings'. However, the earliest extant version of the *Book of Settlements*, compiled by Sturla Thordarson (1214–84), and the *Icelandic Annals* both date Ingolf's arrival to the year 874.

☙

4. THOROLF GOES TO ICELAND

Thorolf Mostur-Beard held a great feast and asked the advice of his friend Thor about what he should do, either make peace with the King, or leave the country and try his luck elsewhere. As it turned out, Thorolf was advised to go to Iceland, so he bought a sizeable ocean-going ship, prepared it for the voyage, then sailed off with his goods, his household, and those of his friends who had decided to go with him. He dismantled the temple, and, along with most of its timbers, put aside some of the earth from under Thor's pedestal.

Thorolf put to sea and had a good passage. He made landfall in the south and sailed west along the coast round Reykja Ness. By the time the fair wind began to fail them, they were able to make out some broad bays cutting into the coast. Thorolf threw overboard the high-seat pillars from the temple with the figure of Thor carved on one of them, and declared that he would settle at any place in Iceland where Thor chose to send the pillars ashore. No sooner had the pillars begun drifting away from the ship than they were swept towards the western bay – not slowly either, from what people could see. Then a breeze sprang up, and Thorolf sailed westward round Snæfell Ness into the bay. They could see it was broad and long, with high mountains on either side, so Thorolf gave a name to it and called it Breida Fjord. He put in to land half-way up on the south side, and where he brought his ship in came to be known later as Hofsvag.[1] Then he began exploring the land. On the tip of the headland to the north of the creek they saw where Thor had come ashore with the pillars. It has been called Thor's Ness ever since. Thorolf carried fire round the land he

---

1. Literally, 'Temple Creek'. Later, according to the story, Thorolf's temple stood near the creek.

claimed, between Staf River in the west and the one he called Thor's River in the east, and settled his crew there.[2]

Thorolf established a great farm at Hofsvag which he called Hofstad, and had a large temple built there with its door in one of the side walls near the gable. Just inside the door stood the high-seat pillars with the so-called holy nails fixed in them, and beyond that point the whole building was considered a sanctuary. Inside the main temple was a structure built much like the choir in churches nowadays, and in the middle a raised platform like an altar. On this platform lay a solid ring weighing twenty ounces, upon which people had to swear all their oaths. It was the business of the temple priest to wear this ring on his arm at every public meeting. There was a sacrificial bowl on the platform too, with a sacrificial twig shaped like a priest's aspergillum for the blood of animals killed as offerings to the gods to be sprinkled from the bowl. Inside the choir-like part of the building the figures of gods were arranged in a circle right round the platform.[3] Every farmer had to pay tax to the temple. Another of their duties was to support the temple priest in his missions, just as farmers nowadays have to support their chieftains. It was the priest's business to see to the temple and maintain it properly at his own expense, as well as hold sacrificial feasts.

Thorolf gave the name Thor's Ness to the region between Vigra Fjord and Hofsvag. On this headland is a mountain held so sacred by Thorolf that no one was allowed even to look at it without first having washed himself, and no living creature on this mountain, neither man nor beast, was to be harmed until it left of its own accord. Thorolf called this mountain Helga

2. The custom of carrying fire round the land claimed is mentioned several times in the *Book of Settlements*, and seems to have been intended to keep evil spirits away.

3. This is the most detailed and circumstantial description of a pagan temple and the sacerdotal functions of the priest-chieftains to be found anywhere in medieval Icelandic literature. Its authenticity, however, is rather doubtful.

Fell[4] and believed that he and his kinsmen would go into it when they died.[5]

Thorolf used to hold all his courts on the point of the headland where Thor had come ashore, and that was where he started the district assembly.[6] This place was so holy that he would let no one desecrate it, either with bloodshed or with excrement; and for a privy they used a special rock in the sea which they called Dritsker.[7]

By now, Thorolf was running his farm in fine style and had a large number of men with him. At that time there was plenty of food to be had both from the islands and from the sea.[8]

☙

5. IN THE HEBRIDES

Now we come back to Bjorn Ketilsson, who had sailed west across the North Sea after his parting from Thorolf Mostur-Beard, which we have already described. By the time he reached the Hebrides, his father Ketil had died, but he met his brother Helgi and their sisters, and they invited him to share in their prosperity. Bjorn discovered they had changed their faith and thought it very weak-minded of them to have renounced the old belief of their forefathers, so he didn't fancy the place and refused to make his home there, though he did spend the winter with his sister Aud and her son Thorstein. When the

4. Literally, 'Holy Mountain'. There are several other Helga Fells in Iceland. The name seems to reflect pre-Christian veneration.
5. See p. 38; and compare *Njal's Saga* (Penguin Classics, 1960), p. 68: 'Some fishermen at Kaldbak thought they had seen Svan being warmly welcomed into the innermost depths of Kaldbakshorn Mountain.'
6. Before the Althing was instituted for the whole of Iceland in 930, there seem to have been two local assemblies: the Thor's Ness Assembly (mentioned here), and the Kjalar Ness Assembly, which was founded by Thorstein Ingolfsson, son of Iceland's first settler.
7. Literally, 'Dirt Skerry'.
8. The sea yielded fish, whales, and seals; the islands sea-fowl and eggs.

family realized that Bjorn intended paying no attention to them, they started calling him Bjorn the Easterner, and thought less of him for having refused to settle there.

☙

6. BJORN GOES TO ICELAND

Bjorn stayed two years in the Hebrides before making ready for his voyage to Iceland. When he left, Hallstein Thorolfsson went with him. They landed in Breida Fjord, and with Thorolf's approval Bjorn took possession of land between Staf River and Hrauns Fjord, building his farm at Borgarholt in Bjorn's Haven. People thought him the finest of men. Hallstein Thorolfsson considered it a slur on his manhood that he should have land granted him by his own father, so he crossed over to the other side of Breida Fjord, staked his claim there, and settled at Hallstein's Ness.

Some years later Aud the Deep-Minded came to Iceland, where she spent her first winter with her brother Bjorn, then took possession of the whole of the Dales between Skrauma River and Dogurdar River, and made her home at Hvamm.[1] By this time all the districts round Breida Fjord had been fully settled. There is no need to record here the settlements of people who do not come into our story.

☙

7. OTHER SETTLERS

A man called Geirrod took possession of land between Thor's River and Langadale, and made his home at Eyr. Ulfar the Champion came to Iceland with Geirrod, who granted him land round Ulfar's Fell, and along with them came Finngeir,

---

1. Aud's settlement is described in some detail in *Laxdæla Saga*, pp. 53–5.

son of Thorstein Ondur, who settled at Alftafjord. He was the
father of Thorfinn, father of Thorbrand of Alftafjord.

A man called Vestar, son of Thorolf Bladderbald, came to
Iceland with his old father and took possession of land west of
Urthvala Fjord. He made his home at Ondurda Eyr, and his
son Asgeir farmed there afterwards.

Bjorn the Easterner was the first of these settlers to die, and a
burial mound was raised over him at Borgarlæk. Two sons
survived him. One of them was Kjallak the Old, who inherited
the farm at Bjorn's Haven after his father's death. His wife was
Astrid, daughter of Hrolf the Chieftain and sister to Steinolf
the Short. Kjallak and Astrid had three children: Thorgrim the
Priest was their only son; and their daughters were Gerd, who
married Thormod the Priest, son of Odd Rakki, and Helga,
who became the wife of Asgeir of Eyr. A great many people are
descended from Kjallak's children, and they are called the
Kjalleklings.

Bjorn's other son was called Ottar. He married a woman
called Gro, daughter of Geirleif and sister to Oddleif of
Barda Strand; and their children were Helgi, father of
Osvif the Wise,[1] Bjorn, father of Vigfus of Drapuhlid, and
Vilgeir.

In his old age Thorolf Mostur-Beard married a woman called
Unn, according to some people the daughter of Thorstein the
Red, though Ari Thorgilsson the Learned does not include her
among Thorstein's children.[2] Thorolf and Unn had a son called
Stein. Thorolf dedicated the boy to his friend Thor and gave
him the name Thorstein. He was a very promising lad, even at
an early age.

Hallstein Thorolfsson married Osk, Thorstein the Red's-

---

1. This Osvif was the father of Gudrun, the principal heroine of *Laxdæla Saga*,
   and is mentioned in Chapters 56 and 64.
2. It is not known to which source this refers. For Ari, see *Laxdæla Saga*, p. 51,
   note 3.

daughter, and they had a son called Thorstein. Thorolf Mostur-Beard brought him up and nicknamed him Thorstein Surt. His own son he called Thorstein the Cod-Biter.

❧

8. THOROLF TWIST-FOOT

About this time Geirrid, sister of Geirrod of Eyr, came to Iceland, and Geirrod granted her land at Borgardale, west of Alfta Fjord. She built a hall right across the main road, and every traveller was expected to pass through it. In the hall stood a table always laden with food which all were welcome to share, and for this people thought her the finest of women.

Geirrid had been married to Bjorn, son of Bolverk Blind-Snout, and they had a son called Thorolf, a great viking. He came out to Iceland some years after his mother and spent his first winter there with her. Thorolf thought the land which his mother had taken not nearly extensive enough, so he challenged Ulfar the Champion to single combat for the land he owned, Ulfar being old and childless. Ulfar chose to die rather than let himself be bullied by Thorolf, and they fought a duel at Alftafjord. Ulfar was killed and Thorolf wounded in the leg, so he walked with a limp for the rest of his life and got the nickname Twist-Foot. Thorolf took over the land that had belonged to Ulfar and set up house at Hvamm in Thorsardale. He was a very harsh man.

Thorolf Twist-Foot sold some land to two freedmen who had belonged to Thorbrand of Alftafjord, Ulfar's Fell to one called Ulfar, and Orlygsstad to one called Orlyg; and there they lived for many a year.

Thorolf had three children, one of them a son, Arnkel. Thorolf's daughter Gunnfrid married Thorbeinir of Thorbeinisstad which stands on Vatnshals east of Drapuhlid. Their sons were Sigmund and Thorgils, and they also had a daughter, Thorgerd, who married Vigfus of Drapuhlid. Thorolf Twist-Foot's second daughter was called Geirrid. She married Thorolf, son of Herjolf Holkinrazi, and they lived at Mavahlid. Their children were Thorarin the Black and Gudny.

❧

9. DESECRATION

When Thorolf Mostur-Beard died at Hofstad, Thorstein Cod-Biter inherited his father's farm, and married Thora, Olaf's-daughter, the sister of Thord Gellir, who was at that time living at Hvamm.[1] A burial mound was raised over Thorolf at Haugsness, west of Hofstad.

By this time the Kjalleklings had grown so puffed up with arrogance they thought themselves better than anyone else in the settlements. Bjorn the Easterner had so many kinsmen there was no family in Breidafjord to compare with his. At that time their kinsman Children-Kjallak was living at a farm in Medalfell Strand, now called Kjallaksstad. He had a good many sons, very able men who supported all their kinsmen on the south side of the bay at assemblies and other public meetings.

One spring at the Thor's Ness Assembly, Thorgrim Kjallaksson and his brother-in-law Asgeir of Eyr declared publicly that they would no longer tolerate the arrogance of the Thorsnessings and meant to ease themselves there on the grass just as they would at any other meeting, even though the Thorsnessings, so full of their own importance, thought their land more sacred than any other in Breidafjord. The Kjalleklings let it be known that they were planning to waste no more shoe-leather on trips to any off-shore skerry whenever they felt the demands of nature. When Thorstein Cod-Biter heard about

---

1. Thord Gellir was one of the leading chieftains in tenth-century Iceland. He figures in *Laxdæla Saga*, *Hen-Thorir's Saga*, and below in Chapter 10.

this, having no intention of allowing them to desecrate the field his father Thorolf held sacred above all his land, he gathered his friends around him with the idea of barring the Kjalleklings from the Assembly Ground by force should they attempt to desecrate it. These were the men who backed Thorstein: Thorgeir the Bent, son of Geirrod of Eyr; the Men of Alftafjord, Thorfinn and his son Thorbrand; Thorolf Twist-Foot, and many friends and followers besides.

That evening, after they had eaten, the Kjalleklings took their weapons and went out to the headland. As soon as Thorstein and his men saw them turning off from the path to the skerry, they ran for their weapons and chased after them shouting challenges and abuse. The Kjalleklings saw them coming, and closed up ready to defend themselves, but the Thorsnessings went for them so fiercely, the Kjalleklings were forced back from the field down on to the beach. There they turned to face their attackers, and the fighting began in real earnest. There were fewer of the Kjalleklings, but they had all the best fighting men.

At this point the men of Skoga Strand, Thorgest the Old and Aslak of Langadale, realized what was happening and hurried over to intervene, but both parties were so incensed there was no separating them until the mediators threatened to join the first side which listened to them. After that the two sides drew apart, on the understanding that the Kjalleklings were not to go back to the Assembly Ground. This meant that they had to board their ship and leave the meeting. There had been deaths on both sides, particularly the Kjalleklings', and many wounded. It was impossible to arrange peace-terms, as neither side was willing to offer them, and each kept threatening to attack the other at the first opportunity. The spot where they fought, where the Thorsnessings had taken their stand, was soaked with blood.

☙

10. TERMS OF SETTLEMENT

After the fight each side kept a standing force, and since feelings were running high between them, friends on both sides decided to send for Thord Gellir, at that time the leading chieftain in Breidafjord. He was a kinsman of the Kjalleklings, but also closely related by marriage to Thorstein, so he seemed the likeliest man to make peace between them. As soon as Thord got word, he set off with a number of men and tried to bring about a settlement, only to find how far they stood from agreement. All the same, he managed to persuade them to agree to a truce and a peace-meeting. As things turned out, it was settled that Thord should arbitrate between them, the Kjalleklings stipulating that never again would they go out to Dritsker to ease themselves, while Thorstein demanded that no Kjalleklings should ever be allowed to defile the Assembly Ground. The Kjalleklings insisted that those of Thorstein's men lost in the skirmish had been killed lawfully, since they themselves had attacked with intent to kill. The Thorsnessings, on the other hand, claimed that because of the outrage committed by the others at a hallowed assembly, it was perfectly lawful for anyone to kill the Kjalleklings. In spite of these conflicting demands, Thord agreed to arbitrate rather than see the two sides part on bad terms.

The first of Thord's decisions was that each side should keep the advantage gained. No compensation was to be paid for the killings and woundings on Thor's Ness. The field, he said, had been defiled by the spilling of blood in enmity, so the ground there was now no holier than any other. He said that those who were the first to attack and shed blood should be held responsible, as they were the ones who broke the peace, and that no assemblies should take place there in future. To ensure their friendship and reconciliation, Thord declared that from then on, Thorgrim Kjallaksson was to bear half the cost of maintaining the temple, and that he and Thorstein were to share the temple dues and the support of the farmers equally between them. Thorgrim was also to back Thorstein in all his lawsuits and safeguard the sanctity of whatever place Thorstein might choose for the new Assembly. One part of the agreement was that Thord Gellir gave his kinswoman Thorhild, daughter of his neighbour Thorkel Meinakur, in marriage to Thorgrim Kjallaksson, who from then on was known as Thorgrim the Priest.

This was when they moved the Assembly to the east side of the headland, where it is still held; and when Thord Gellir instituted the Quarter Courts,[1] he decided that the Court for the West Quarter – that is for all the people in the West Fjords – should meet there too. The circle where the court used to sentence people to be sacrificed can still be seen, with Thor's Stone inside it on which the victims' backs were broken, and you can still see the blood on the stone.[2]

Though this assembly place was held to be highly sacred, people were not forbidden to ease themselves there.

ᛟ

11. THORSTEIN COD-BITER DIES

Thorstein Cod-Biter ran his farm in fine style, and used to have thirty free men working for him. He was a generous provider and often went out fishing. Thorstein established the farm at Helgafell, and when he moved house there, his

1. According to Ari Thorgilsson (*Book of Icelanders*, Chapter 5), it was at the suggestion of Thord Gellir that Iceland was divided into four Quarters for judicial purposes. The Quarter Courts dealt with lawsuits between litigants from different local assemblies, but belonging to the same Quarter. See *Njal's Saga*, pp. 54, 298–300.
2. This is one of the few references to human sacrifice in pagan Iceland.

temple made it a place of the greatest importance. He took pains over the building of another farm on the headland near the place where the Assembly had been held. This he gave to his kinsman Thorstein Surt, who lived there afterwards and had a great reputation for shrewdness.

Thorstein Cod-Biter had a son called Bork the Stout. Then in the summer when Thorstein was twenty-five years old, Thora gave birth to another son, who was sprinkled with water and given the name Grim. Thorstein dedicated this boy to Thor, calling him Thorgrim, and said he should become a temple priest.

That same autumn Thorstein went to Hoskuld Island to fetch provisions. One evening in the autumn as Thorstein's shepherd was tending sheep north of Helga Fell, he saw the whole north side of the mountain opened up, with great fires burning inside it and the noise of feasting and clamour over the ale-horns. As he strained to catch particular words, he was able to make out that Thorstein Cod-Biter and his crew were being welcomed into the mountain, and that Thorstein was being invited to sit in the place of honour opposite his father.

That evening the shepherd told Thorstein's wife Thora about this apparition. She was deeply disturbed by it and said it could be a foreboding of something very sinister. In the morning some men brought news from Hoskuld Island that Thorstein Cod-Biter had been drowned on a fishing trip. People thought it a bitter loss.

Thora kept the farm and took on an overseer called Hallvard to help her to run it. She had a son by him, called Mar.

12. A NEW GENERATION

The sons of Thorstein Cod-Biter grew up with their mother, both promising men, though Thorgrim outstripped his brother in every way. As soon as he was old enough, he became a temple priest. Thorgrim married Thordis, Sur's-daughter, in Dyrafjord and went to live there in the west with his brothers-in-law, Gisli and Thorkel. Thorgrim killed Vestein Vesteinsson at an autumn feast at Haukadale, and the following autumn when he was twenty-five years old, the very age his father had been when he was drowned, Thorgrim's brother-in-law Gisli killed him at an autumn feast at Sæbol. A few days later Thorgrim's widow Thordis gave birth to a boy, called Thorgrim after his father. A little later Thordis married her brother-in-law Bork the Stout and went to live with him at Helgafell,[1] but her son Thorgrim was sent to Alftafjord to be fostered by Thorbrand. Thorgrim was a very difficult child, so they called him Snerrir, and afterwards Snorri.[2]

Thorbrand of Alftafjord married Thurid, daughter of Thorfinn Sel-Thorisson from Raudamel, and these were their children: Thorleif Kimbi the eldest, the next Snorri, the third Thorodd, the fourth Thorfinn, the fifth Thormod; and there was a daughter as well, called Thorgerd. All of Thorbrand's sons were blood-brothers to Snorri Thorgrimsson.

At that time Arnkel, Thorolf Twist-Foot's son, was living at

1. This is a concise summary of the central plot of the tragic *Gisli's Saga*, which the author of *Eyrbyggja Saga* had evidently read. Vestein was Gisli's brother-in-law and blood-brother. According to *Gisli's Saga* it was Gisli's sister Thordis who, having discovered that he had killed her husband, urged her brother-in-law Bork the Stout to take revenge, after she had become his wife.
2. *Gisli's Saga* gives a similar account of the origin of Snorri's name. The words *snerrir* and *snorri* are cognates and have similar meanings: a turbulent, warlike man.

Bolstad near Vadilshofdi, a big strong fellow, clever at law and very shrewd. He was a great-hearted man and stood head and shoulders above all the other men in the district both in popularity and strength of character. Arnkel was a temple priest and had plenty of support.

As we have said, Thorgrim Kjallaksson was living at Bjorn's Haven. He had three sons by his wife Thorhild. Brand, the eldest, lived at Kross Ness near Brimlar Head. The second, Arngrim, was a tall strong man, big-boned and ginger-haired, with a prominent nose. He had gone bald at the temples while still young, his eyebrows met but his eyes were large and fine. He was a very arrogant man and unjust, which got him the name Styr.[3] Thorgrim's youngest son was Vermund, a tall man, slim and handsome, so people called him Vermund the Slender.

Asgeir of Eyr had a son called Thorlak who married Thurid, daughter of Audun Stoti of Hraunsfjord, and their children were Steinthor, Bergthor, Thormod, Thord Blig, and Helga. Steinthor was the most promising of Thorlak's children. He was tall and strong, a skilled fighting-man of outstanding ability, but normally very quiet. Steinthor had been singled out as one of the three best fighters in Iceland, the other two being Helgi Droplaugarson and Vermund Fringe.[4] Thormod was shrewd and self-controlled, Thord Blig hot-tempered and outspoken. Bergthor, the youngest, also showed great promise.

3. *Styr* means a 'battle, skirmish', etc.
4. These heroes figure in *The Droplaugarsons' Saga* and the *Reykdæla Saga* respectively.

☙

13. SNORRI TRAVELS TO NORWAY

Snorri Thorgrimsson was fourteen years old when he went abroad with his blood-brothers, Thorleif Kimbi and Thorodd. His uncle Bork the Stout advanced him fifty ounces of silver for travelling expenses. They had a good passage, got to Norway in the autumn, and spent the winter in Rogaland, where Snorri stayed with Erling Skjalgsson of Sola. Erling treated him well because of the old friendship between their forebears, Horda-Kari and Thorolf Mostur-Beard.

The following summer they were late getting ready to sail back to Iceland, but after a difficult passage they reached Horna Fjord just before winter. As these men of Breidafjord came ashore people saw a world of difference between the outfit of Snorri and that of Thorleif Kimbi. Thorleif had bought the best horse he could get, along with an elaborate, painted saddle. He carried an ornamented sword, a gold-inlaid spear, and a dark-blue, heavily gilded shield. All his clothes were of the finest quality, and it was on this outfit that he'd spent most of his travelling money. Snorri, on the other hand, was wearing a black cloak and was riding a fine black mare. He had an old trough-shaped saddle, and his weapons were not much to look at. Thorodd's outfit came somewhere in between.

They rode through Sida and so by the usual route west to Borgarfjord, then across Fletir and stayed the night at Alfta-fjord. Next day Snorri rode over to Helgafell hoping to spend the winter there, but Bork was against it. Everybody made fun of Snorri because of his outfit, and Bork said he must have had bad luck with his money to lose it all.

One day early in winter twelve men fully armed walked into the living-room at Helgafell. Their leader was Bork's kinsman, Eyjolf the Grey, Thord Gellir's son, who was living west at Otradale in Arnarfjord. When people asked the news, they

announced the killing of Gisli Sursson, and named those he
had killed before he died. This was good news to Bork,[1] and he
told Thordis and Snorri to give a hearty welcome to Eyjolf, the
man having rid the family name of an ugly blemish.

Snorri had little to say about it, and Thordis said it would be
welcome enough 'if gruel were given to the killer of Gisli'.

'It wasn't food I had in mind,' said Bork.

He showed Eyjolf to the seat of honour, then settled the
others below him. The visitors laid their weapons on the floor.
Bork was sitting next to Eyjolf on the far side, and after him,
Snorri.

Thordis began carrying in the porridge-bowls with the
spoons in them, and while she was serving Eyjolf she dropped
one of the spoons. As she stooped to pick it up, she grabbed
hold of Eyjolf's sword and made a quick thrust with it under
the table. It pierced Eyjolf in the thigh, but the pommel caught
the table, checking the blow. All the same it was a nasty
wound.

Bork shoved the table away from him and hit out at Thordis,
but Snorri pushed Bork back away from her so hard that he fell.
Snorri put his arms round his mother and set her down beside
him. He said her sorrows were great enough without her being
beaten as well. Eyjolf and his men were on their feet and had to
be forcibly held back. The outcome was that Bork gave Eyjolf
the right to decide how much compensation should be paid.
He awarded himself a large sum for the wound, and then rode
off. All this only served to aggravate the bad feeling between
Bork and Snorri.

1. This refers to *Gisli's Saga*, a complex family vendetta (see p. 11 of Introduction). Gisli is the killer of Bork's brother and Snorri's father, but also
   Thordis's dearly loved brother and Snorri's maternal uncle.

❧

14. SNORRI WINS HELGAFELL

In the spring at the District Assembly, Snorri demanded his inheritance from Bork. Bork told him he was quite ready to hand it over.

'However,' he said, 'I'm not going to the trouble of dividing Helgafell. I can see we're not the kind of men to share the estate, so I'm going to buy you out and keep it for myself.'

'I'd think it more reasonable,' said Snorri, 'if you'd value the farm yourself and leave me to decide who's going to do the buying out.'

Bork thought this over and couldn't see how Snorri would ever have enough ready cash to pay for the farm, so he valued the estate at sixty ounces of silver, not including the islands as he expected to be able to buy them up cheaply if Snorri got another farm. He also stipulated that the money should be handed over on the spot and the buyer not allowed to get himself into any man's debt in order to pay.

'Now, Snorri, it's up to you,' said Bork. 'You'd better make up your mind here and now.'

'It's obvious, Bork,' said Snorri, 'you must think me very short of money when you set such a low price on Helgafell. But I've decided to take my father's estate at this price, so give me your hand, and let's seal the bargain.'

'I'm not doing that till every penny's been paid,' said Bork.

Snorri turned to Thorbrand, his foster-father. 'Didn't I give you a money-purse last autumn?' he asked.

'Yes, you did,' said Thorbrand, and pulled out the purse from under his cloak. They counted the silver, and even after they had paid out every penny for the estate, there were still sixty ounces of silver left in the purse. Bork took the money and formally handed over the ownership of the estate to Snorri.

'Your purse turned out to be fuller than I'd expected, kinsman,' said Bork. 'Now I'd like us to forget the bad feeling that's grown up between us, and to show my good faith I'll give you a hand, and share in the running of the farm with you for the next year. After all, you've not much in the way of livestock.'

'You can keep your livestock,' said Snorri, 'and clear out of Helgafell.' And the way Snorri wanted it was the way it had to be.

When Bork was about to leave, his wife Thordis came forward and declared in the presence of witnesses that she was divorcing him on the grounds that he had struck her, and she would not let herself be knocked about by him any more. A division of their property was made, with Snorri acting for his mother, since he was her heir. Bork was forced to accept for himself what he had meant for others, getting very little for the islands.

After that Bork left Helgafell, and settled over in Medalfell Strand. He farmed first at Barkarstad between Orrahvall and Tongue, but later moved to Glerarwood, and there he lived till he was an old man.

☙

15. SNORRI THE PRIEST

Snorri Thorgrimsson began farming at Helgafell, with his mother in charge of the household. Mar Hallvardsson, his uncle, moved in with ample livestock and became the overseer. Snorri was soon running his farm in fine style, with plenty of men to follow him.

Snorri was of medium height and rather slight build, a handsome, regular-featured man with a fair complexion, flaxen hair, and a reddish beard. He was usually eventempered, and it was hard to tell whether he was pleased or not. He was a very shrewd man with unusual foresight, a long memory, and a taste for vengeance. To his friends he gave good counsel, but his enemies learned to fear the advice he gave. As Snorri was now in charge of the temple, he was called Snorri the Priest. He became a man of great power and some people envied him bitterly, for there were plenty who thought themselves just as well-born, with a better claim to distinction, lacking neither followers nor proof of their fighting spirit.

Bork the Stout and Thordis had a daughter called Thurid. She married Thorbjorn the Stout of Frodriver, son of Orm the Slender who lived there before him and was the first man to settle at Frodriver. Thorbjorn had been married before to Thurid, daughter of Asbrand of Kamb in Breidavik and sister of Bjorn the Breidavik-Champion, who was later to play his part in the story, and Arnbjorn the Strong. The sons of Thurid and Thorbjorn were Ketil the Champion, Gunnlaug and Hallstein. Thorbjorn thought a lot of himself, and gave lesser men a hard time.

At this time Geirrid, Thorolf Twist-Foot's-daughter, and her son, Thorarin the Black, were living at Mavahlid. He was a big strong fellow, ugly to look at and taciturn, but normally very quiet, with the reputation of being a man of peace. Thorarin was not a wealthy man, but he had a valuable farm. He was so anxious not to get involved in things, his enemies said there was as much of the woman in him as there was man. He was married to a woman called Aud, and had a sister, Gudny, married to Vermund the Slender.

A widow called Katla lived at Holt, west of Mavahlid. She was a fine-looking woman, but not very popular, and had a son called Odd, a big robust man, loud-mouthed, a born trouble-maker and given to gossip and slander.

Thorbjorn the Stout's son, Gunnlaug, had a passion for knowledge, and often went over to Mavahlid to study witchcraft with Geirrid Thorolf's-daughter, she being a woman who knew a thing or two. One day, when Gunnlaug was on his way over to Mavahlid, he called in at Holt and had a long talk with

Katla. She asked him whether he was off to Mavahlid again 'to stroke the old hag up the belly.'

Gunnlaug said that was not why he was going there. 'Are you so young yourself Katla,' he added, 'that you can afford to talk of Geirrid's age?'

'I wouldn't dream of making comparisons,' said Katla. 'But that's neither here nor there. You may not be able to think about anybody but Geirrid, but she isn't the only woman with a few ideas in her head.'

Odd Katlason often went over with Gunnlaug to Mavahlid. Whenever they were late coming back, Katla used to invite Gunnlaug to stay the night, but he always went straight home.

☙

16. GUNNLAUG'S MISHAP

One day early in the first winter that Snorri farmed at Helgafell, it happened that Gunnlaug Thorbjarnarson and Odd Katlason went over to Mavahlid. Gunnlaug and Geirrid spent most of the day talking together.

'I wish you wouldn't go back home tonight,' she said to him late in the evening, 'there are too many sea-spirits about, and many a fair skin hides a foul mind. Anyway, you don't have the look of a lucky man about you just now.'

'Nothing is going to happen to me,' said Gunnlaug, 'not while there's two of us together.'

'Odd won't be any use to you,' she said, 'you'll end up paying for your stubbornness.'

At that, Gunnlaug and Odd walked away from the farm, and over to Holt. Katla had gone to bed when they arrived there, and she asked Odd to invite Gunnlaug to stay the night. He said he'd already asked him, 'but he insists on going home'.

'Let him go, then,' she said, 'and face what's coming to him.'

Gunnlaug didn't come home that evening, and there was talk about making a search for him, but nothing came of it. During the night Thorbjörn looked outside and saw his son lying unconscious by the door. They carried him in and pulled off his clothes. He was scratched all over the shoulders and the flesh had been ripped to the bone. His injuries kept him in bed for the rest of the winter. There was a lot of talk about his illness, and Odd Katlason maintained that Geirrid must have bewitched him and ridden him for having taken such short leave of her that evening. Most people agreed that this was what must have happened.

In the spring at Summons Days,[1] Thorbjorn rode over to Mavahlid and served a summons on Geirrid for being a night-witch and causing Gunnlaug bodily harm. The case was heard at the Thor's Ness Assembly. Snorri the Priest supported his brother-in-law Thorbjorn, and Arnkel the Priest acted on behalf of his sister Geirrid. A jury of twelve was appointed to try the case. Because of their kinship with plaintiff and defendant, neither Snorri nor Arnkel was qualified to testify, and Helgi the Priest of Hofgardar, father of Bjorn, father of Gest, father of Poet-Ref, was chosen to give the verdict. Arnkel the Priest approached the court and swore an oath on the altar ring that Geirrid was not responsible for Gunnlaug's injuries, and Thorarin along with ten other men took the same oath. Then Helgi announced the jury's finding that there was no case to answer, and the charge preferred by Snorri and Thorbjorn was dismissed. The outcome was a great setback to them.

---

1. The last days for serving a district-court summons were two weeks before the court convened.

☙

17. ILLUGI THE BLACK

At the same Assembly Thorgrim Kjallaksson and his sons
quarrelled with Illugi the Black over the dowry of Illugi's wife
Ingibjorg, Asbjorn's-daughter, which Tin-Forni had charge of.
A fierce gale sprang up during the Assembly, and no one from
Medalfell Strand could get through. It was a serious blow to
Thorgrim that his kinsmen could not be present. Illugi had a
hundred and twenty men with him, all good fighters, and
pressed his claim hard. The Kjalleklings went to court with the
idea of breaking it up, and a mob began to form, but people
forced their way in and separated the two sides. In the end,
after Illugi had argued the matter out with him, Tin-Forni
handed over the money.

This is what the poet Odd says in his eulogy on Illugi:

> At Thor's Ness the crowds
> crushed west to the court
> when the bold fighter
> freely won a fortune:
> Forni's gold fell
> purse-packed, to the feeder
> of ravenous ravens,
> hard-won peace followed rage.

But later, when the gale had blown itself out and the
Kjalleklings were able to cross over from Medalfell Strand,
Thorgrim Kjallaksson refused to honour the settlement and
made an attack on Illugi. When fighting began in earnest,
Snorri the Priest asked people to help calm things down, and
managed to get a truce agreed between them. The Kjalleklings
lost three men in the battle, and Illugi four. Styr Thorgrimsson
himself killed two men there. Odd has this to say about it in his
eulogy on Illugi:

> Pledged to keep peace,
> they dishonoured their promise,
> three fierce sword-flourishers
> struck down in the fight.
> Snorri, seasoned in battle,
> settled the bitter business,
> well-earned the honour
> for wielding power ably.

Illugi thanked Snorri the Priest for all he had done and asked him to accept a fee, but Snorri said he wanted no payment for his help this time, though when Illugi invited him home, Snorri accepted. Illugi gave him some fine gifts, and for a time they stayed on friendly terms.

☙

18. HOSTILITIES

In the summer Thorgrim Kjallaksson died, and his son Vermund the Slender took over the farm at Bjorn's Haven. He was a shrewd man, and his advice was always sound. At that time Styr had been farming for a while nearby at Hraun, east of Bjorn's Haven. Styr, an intelligent and ruthless man, married Thorbjorg, Thorstein Sleet-Nose's-daughter, and their sons were Thorstein and Hall. They also had a daughter, Asdis, a fine woman, but rather proud-spirited. Styr lorded it over his neighbours and had plenty of men with him. He was involved in many disputes, as he had killed a number of men without paying compensation.

That summer a ship from overseas put in at Salteyrar Mouth. Some Norwegians owned a half-share in it, and their captain Bjorn went to stay the winter with Steinthor of Eyr. The other share belonged to a group of Hebrideans, and their captain, Alfgeir, went to Mavahlid and stayed with Thorarin the Black. Alfgeir had a companion called Nagli lodging there too, a man of Scottish origins, well-built and a speedy runner.

Eyrbyggja Saga

Thorarin kept a fine fighting stallion up in the mountains, and Thorbjorn the Stout had a herd of stud-horses he left to graze on the mountain pasture, though he used to pick out some of them every autumn for slaughtering. It happened that Thorbjorn's horses could not be found though people searched far and wide for them. The weather was very bad that autumn.

At the beginning of winter Thorbjorn sent Odd Katlason over to Hraun south across the moor, where a man called Spa-Gils was living at the time. He had second sight and was very clever when it came to investigating thefts or anything else which needed straightening out. Odd asked him about Thorbjorn's horses: had they been stolen by foreigners, by people from other districts, or by Thorbjorn's own neighbours?

'Tell Thorbjorn exactly what I'm going to tell you,' said Spa-Gils. 'I don't think his horses have strayed far from their usual pasture, and it's hard to fix the blame. Better to bear one's losses than stir up a lot of trouble.'

When Odd came back to Frodriver, Thorbjorn and his men thought that the message from Spa-Gils hinted at the people of Mavahlid. Odd went on to suggest that Spa-Gils had meant something else, namely that the ones most likely to have stolen the horses would be those who were worst off for money and now had extra mouths to feed. It seemed to Thorbjorn that this could only refer to the men of Mavahlid.

Thorbjorn set off with eleven men. One of them was his son Hallstein, but his other son, Ketil the Champion, was abroad at the time. Another member of the party was Thorir Arnarson of Arnarhvall, Thorbjorn's neighbour and a great fighting man. Odd Katlason came with him too. First they went over to Holt. Katla dressed her son Odd in a reddish-brown tunic she had just made. From there they rode to Mavahlid. When they arrived, Thorarin was standing outside the door with his servants. They had seen the men coming up, and greeted Thorbjorn, asking him the news.

'We've come here to look for the horses stolen from me in the autumn,' said Thorbjorn. 'I mean to search your premises.'

'Have you a proper warrant?' asked Thorarin. 'Have you appointed lawful witnesses to be present? What guarantees can you give for our safety while you're searching? Have you searched anywhere else?'

'I don't think there'll be any need to search elsewhere,' said Thorbjorn.

'If you're not prepared to go about it legally,' said Thorarin, 'I forbid you to search my premises.'

'Then we'll take it you're guilty,' said Thorbjorn, 'or you'd not have stopped us searching.'

'All right, do whatever you like,' said Thorarin.

Thorbjorn named six men to act as jury for the door-court,[1] and charged Thorarin with stealing the horses. Just then Geirrid came through the door and saw what was going on.

'It's true what they say about you, Thorarin,' she said. 'You're more like a woman than a man, putting up as you do with all Thorbjorn's insults. I can't think what I ever did to have a son like you.'

Then Alfgeir the ship's-captain said, 'We'll back you in every way we can, whatever you decide.'

'I'm not standing around here any longer,' said Thorarin, and rushed forward with his men, meaning to break up the court. There were seven of them, and at once fighting broke out. Thorarin killed one of Thorbjorn's servants and Alfgeir another, then Thorarin lost one of his men as well, but no weapon could bite Odd Katlason. Thorarin's wife Aud called on the women to separate the fighters, and they began throwing clothes on to the men's weapons. Then Thorarin and his party went back into the house. Threatening to raise the matter at the Thor's Ness Assembly, Thorbjorn rode over to the other side of the creek with his men. They dressed their wounds at a place called Korngard, beside a fenced-in haystack.

1. Door-courts (*duradómar*) are not mentioned in the Icelandic laws; and it has been suggested that *Eyrbyggja Saga* may here preserve the memory of a judicial practice which went early out of use.

After the fight a human hand was found in the home
meadow where they had clashed at Mavahlid. Somebody
showed the hand to Thorarin, and he saw it was a woman's.
He asked for Aud and was told she'd gone to bed. He went to
see her and asked her had she been hurt, but Aud told him not
to fuss. Then he saw her hand had been cut off. Thorarin called
out to his mother to come and dress the wound, then ran out of
the house with his men to chase after Thorbjorn. As they came
up to the haystack, they could hear Thorbjorn and his men
talking away. Hallstein was speaking.

'Thorarin cleared himself today of that slur on his manhood,' he said.

'He fought like a real man,' said Thorbjorn. 'But then, even
though people may normally be quite different, most act
bravely when they're in a corner.'

'Thorarin may be brave,' said Odd, 'but people won't think
him very clever to have chopped off his wife's hand.'

'Is that true?' asked Thorbjorn.

'True as daylight,' said Odd.

They all began falling about, laughing and joking. Just at
that moment Thorarin and his men came up with them. Nagli
was the first to get close, but when he saw them brandishing
their weapons, he lost his nerve and began racing up the
hillside, scared out of his wits. Thorarin made for Thorbjorn
and with a sword-cut split his head right down to the jaw.
Then Thorir Arnarson and two others set upon Thorarin,
Hallstein and a companion tackled Alfgeir, and Odd went with
another man against one of Alfgeir's shipmates. Three of
Thorbjorn's men made a fierce attack on two of Thorarin's.
Then Thorarin sliced through Thorir's leg at the thick of the calf
and killed both his companions. Hallstein was cut down by
Alfgeir and mortally wounded. As soon as Thorarin was free,
Odd Katlason took to his heels, and two others ran off after
him. Odd was unharmed as no weapon could bite into his
tunic. The rest of Thorbjorn's men lay behind on the
battlefield, and both of Thorarin's servants were dead.

Thorarin and his men took Thorbjorn's horses and rode home. On their way back they could see Nagli running along high up on the hillside, and by the time they reached the home meadow, Nagli had gone past the farmstead and was heading straight for Buland Head. There he met two of Thorarin's slaves chasing sheep away from the edge of the cliff. He told them about the fighting and the odds, and said he knew for certain that Thorarin and all his men must be dead by now. Just as he was telling them this, they saw men riding over the meadow. Thorarin and his companions badly wanted to rescue Nagli and make sure he didn't jump over the cliff or dive into the sea, so they spurred their horses and raced towards him. When Nagli and the slaves saw the men riding so hard, they took them for Thorbjorn and his companions, so they set off running towards the cliff till they came to a place now called Slaves' Scree, where Thorarin and his men caught up with the exhausted Nagli: but the slaves jumped off the cliff and were killed, as you would expect. No living creature could survive a fall from that height.

Then Thorarin and his men went home. Geirrid met them at the door and asked what had happened. Thorarin replied with a verse:

> In the court of weapons
> they called me a coward:
> I defended my honour,
> fought, fed the eagles.
> My sword bears witness,
> put to the war-test:
> but I don't care to boast –
> bloodshed's not my business.

'Are you telling me Thorbjorn's been killed?' asked Geirrid. This was Thorarin's answer:

> My sharp edge hewed
> hard below the helm,
> hot blood flowed
> from the fierce fighting man,
> sluiced out in two streams
> from the ears, each side,
> wetting the word-dry mouth:
> my war-stroke the weightier!

'My words gave you an edge, then,' said she. 'Come in and let's see to your wounds.' And that's what they did.

Now we go back to Odd Katlason, who went on his way to Frodriver and told people the news. The widow Thurid gathered men to fetch the dead and wounded. Thorbjorn was laid in a burial mound, but his son Hallstein recovered, as did Thorir of Arnarhvall, though he walked with a wooden leg for the rest of his life, and that got him the nickname Wood-Leg. He married Thorgrima Witch-Face, and their sons were Orn and Val, both sturdy fellows.

❧

19. AFTER THE FIGHT

Thorarin spent the night at home in Mavahlid, and next morning Aud asked him what he planned to do. 'I don't want to turn you out,' she said, 'but I'm afraid there will be more door-courts this winter. One thing I know for certain: Snorri means to do something about the killing of his brother-in-law Thorbjorn.'

Thorarin said:

> Could I catch the eye
> of one keen warrior,
> no crafty law-cracker
> would ever cause my outlawry:
> famished ravens will feast
> on the flesh of men –
> I value Vermund
> and praise his valour!

'Yes, that would be the sensible thing to do,' said Geirrid, 'to ask for the help of such kinsmen as Vermund. Or perhaps from my brother, Arnkel.'

'It's more than likely we'll be needing both before all this is over,' said Thorarin. 'But first I'll go and see what Vermund can do for us.'

That day, all those who had a hand in the killings rode off east along the fjords and arrived at Bjorn's Haven in the evening. They walked straight into the living-room, where all the household was sitting. Vermund greeted them, and, quickly making room for them on the high-seat, he asked Thorarin and his men to sit down. When they had done so, Vermund asked the news. Thorarin said:

> Hear the truth, turn
> your ear to my tale
> in this troubled age
> of ill-temper and turmoil:
> shield-bearers, skilled in war,
> shook their spears at me,
> blades borne in hand
> I saw, bloodstained.

'Can you tell me any more about it, kinsman?' asked Vermund. Thorarin went on:

> Raging were the warriors
> but we destroyed them:
> my sword flashed in the face
> of the shield-bearing foe:
> we laid about us, left
> them little choice –
> yet I favoured friendship
> till they forced my hand.

Gudny, his sister, took the floor. 'Have you cleared your name of the charge of cowardice they were making against you?' she asked. Thorarin said:

> Slander forced me
> to defend my fame.
> Ravens feasted then,
> fattened by the spear's lust:
> busy, the blade rang
> battering my helm;
> blood-tides surged
> like surf at my side.

'It looks as if you didn't waste any time before you took them on,' said Vermund. Thorarin replied:

> Steel-piercing shafts
> screaming songs of battle
> swooped upon my helm
> and gold-rimmed shield:

> my glittering screen
> stained red with gore-paint,
> the battle-plain soaked
> crimson in the blood-storm.

'Did they find out for sure whether you're a man or a woman?' asked Vermund. Thorarin said:

> Accused of cowardice,
> cleared now, my name:
> dead my adversary,
> struck down by my arms.
> Snorri may whisper
> sweet words to his women,
> I've run my eye over ravens
> as they ravaged the dead.

After that Thorarin gave an account of what had happened. Vermund asked: 'Why did you go after them? Didn't you think enough had been done already?' Thorarin said:

> Soon I'll be accused,
> they'll call me a killer:
> gone the sweet seasons
> I set out a-sailing.
> False cowards, they cried
> that I'd cut off my wife's hand,
> jested and jeered, when
> all I sought was justice.

'You've every reason not to stand for their making fun of you,' said Vermund. 'Tell me, what kind of service did the foreigners give you?' Thorarin replied:

> The grovelling Nagli,
> little gave he to glut
> hungry ravens as he ran
> snivelling up the ridge:
> as for helmed Alfgeir,
> eager for the war-play
> was the warrior, wielding
> his steel-bright weapons.

'So Nagli didn't show up too well?' asked Vermund.
Thorarin went on:

> The targe-bearer took off
> in tears from the battle-field;
> fearing for his headpiece,
> he fled in fright
> from danger: all he desired
> was to dive in the ocean,
> to drown the fear
> in his faltering heart.

After Thorarin had spent the night at Bjorn's Haven, Vermund had a word with him. 'You'll probably think me rather
mean and not very keen to help you, kinsman,' he said, 'but I
don't think I'm powerful enough to offer you shelter unless
there are others who are ready to share in these troubles, so
we'd better ride over to Bolstad today. We'll see your kinsman
Arnkel, and find out what help he's willing to give. I don't
think Snorri the Priest will be easy to deal with in this lawsuit.'

'I leave it all to you,' said Thorarin. While they were on their
way, he made this verse:

> Merry the times
> our minds remember,
> the days ere these hands
> dealt Thorbjorn his death-stroke:
> I must run from the rage
> I've aroused in the proud one:
> I loathe the strife
> of the scarlet shield-wall.

This was meant as a hint to Snorri the Priest. So Vermund
and Thorarin rode on their way till they came to Bolstad.
Arnkel gave them a good welcome and asked the news.
Thorarin said:

> Fighting fills me
> with fear and loathing,

> when fiery blades flay
> the flesh from the bone:
> shimmering spears
> sliced through our moon-shields,
> the blade-edge battered
> and beat our breastplates.

Arnkel asked Thorarin to tell him more about the matter. After he had described what had happened, Arnkel said, 'You must have got into quite a rage, kinsman, you're normally so quiet.' Thorarin said:

> People pictured me
> as a man of peace,
> for I tried to beat back
> the powers of bitterness,
> but worthy ways
> can still lead us to war,
> soon the worldly, gay widow
> will understand my words.

'Perhaps you're right,' said Arnkel, 'but kinsman, why not stay with me till this whole affair has been settled one way or the other. Even though I've taken Thorarin under my wing, Vermund, I'd like you to continue giving your support.'

'It's my duty to help Thorarin in every way I can,' said Vermund. 'Even though you've taken charge of the case, my responsibility is just the same.'

'I think it would be best,' said Arnkel, 'for us to stay here together over the winter, close to Snorri the Priest.' And that's what they did.

Arnkel had plenty of men with him that winter. Vermund spent part of the time home at Bjorn's Haven and part with Arnkel. Thorarin had little to say for himself, and his mood never changed. Arnkel was a charming host, always good-tempered. He wanted others to be as happy as himself, and often told Thorarin he should cheer up and not worry so much. He said the widow of Frodriver, so he heard, was taking her loss remarkably well, 'and she'll think it silly of you if you don't act like a man'. Thorarin replied:

> She won't boast at the beer-feast
> that I fear to see blood run,
> the merry widow, when
> I've watched the ravens,
> the birds of prey,
> peck at their pleasure,
> as hard men harvest
> hatred on the field.

One of Arnkel's servants said, 'You'll have to wait till after the Thor's Ness Assembly in the spring before you can decide how to rid yourself of your troubles.' Thorarin replied:

> They say we'll suffer
> setbacks in court;
> we must plead for support
> from powerful chieftains:
> but Arnkel will argue
> an eloquent case,
> he'll sway judge and jury –
> I have faith in justice.

☙

20. SORCERERS PUT TO DEATH

Geirrid of Mavahlid sent word to Bolstad that she had found it was Odd Katlason who had chopped off Aud's hand. She said she had learned this from Aud herself, and more, that Odd had been boasting about it to his friends. When Thorarin and Arnkel heard the story, they set out from home twelve strong and rode over to Mavahlid. They spent the night there and in the morning rode on to Holt. People there saw them coming, but Odd was the only man at home just then. Katla was sitting in the living-room, spinning, and told Odd to sit down beside her. 'Keep quiet,' she said, 'and sit still.'

She told the women to stay in their usual seats. 'And keep quiet,' she said, 'I'll do all the talking.'

Arnkel and his men came up to the farmstead and went straight in. As they walked into the living-room, Katla greeted them and asked the news. Arnkel said he had none to speak of and asked for Odd. Katla said he had gone south to Breidavik, 'but if he were at home, he wouldn't try to avoid you,' she said. 'We've no doubt about your being men of principle.'

'That's as may be,' said Arnkel, 'but we're going to search the house.'

'Just as you wish,' said Katla, and told her housekeeper to carry a light for them and open the store-room. 'It's the only locked room in the house,' she added.

All they could see was Katla spinning yarn on her distaff. They searched all over the house but found no sign of Odd, so off they went. After they had gone a little way, Arnkel stopped in his tracks. 'I wonder,' he asked, 'could Katla have used her witchcraft to make fools of us? Could it be that the thing we thought was a distaff was really her son Odd?'

'That would be just like her,' said Thorarin, 'let's go back.' And that's what they did. When the people at Holt saw them coming back, Katla said to the women, 'You stay in the room where you are. Odd and I are going outside.'

As they left the room, she slipped into the vestibule beside the door and started combing and trimming Odd's hair. Arnkel and his men came rushing inside, and all they could see was Katla playing around with a goat. She seemed to be trimming its forelock and beard and combing its wool. Arnkel and his men went into the living-room but still couldn't see Odd anywhere, and Katla's distaff was lying on the bench. After they made sure Odd had not been hiding there, they walked out of the house and left.

They came to the spot where they had turned back before.

Then Arnkel said, 'Don't you think it could have been Odd masquerading as a goat?'

'Who knows?' said Thorarin. 'Let's turn back quickly and get hold of Katla.'

'We'll give it another try,' said Arnkel, 'and see what happens.' So once again they turned back.

When Katla saw them coming up, she told Odd to take a walk with her. They went outside over to the rubbish-heap, and she told him to lie down beside it. 'Stay here whatever happens,' she said.

Arnkel and his men came up to the farmstead and rushed into the living-room. Katla was sitting on the dais, spinning. She greeted them and said they were becoming quite regular callers, which Arnkel had to admit. His companions grabbed the distaff and started chopping it up.

'Now that you've broken my distaff,' said Katla, 'you'll be able to tell your people back home tonight that your visit to Holt wasn't entirely wasted.'

Arnkel and his men searched for Odd inside and out and could find no living creature except for Katla's pet hog lying by the rubbish-dump, so they went away.

When they were half-way to Mavahlid, Geirrid came to meet them with one of her servants and asked how they'd got on. Thorarin told her what had happened.

She said they hadn't made a proper search for Odd: 'I want you to go back once more, and this time I'm coming with you. There's no point in dealing gently with Katla.'

So they turned back. Geirrid was wearing a blue cloak. The people at Holt saw them coming, and Katla was told there were now fourteen of them, one in bright-coloured clothes.

'That must be Geirrid the witch,' said Katla, 'and this means that something more than sorcery's needed.'

She stood up on the dais and lifted the cushions where she had been sitting. There was a trapdoor in the floor with a hollow place underneath. She told Odd to get down into it, and then arranged everything as it had been before. As she sat down, she told them a strange feeling had come over her.

Arnkel and his party came into the room, and this time there were no greetings. Geirrid threw off her cloak, went up to Katla, and pulled a sealskin bag over her head. Her companions tied the bag firmly round Katla's neck. Then Geirrid told the men to break open the floor, and there they found Odd and tied him up. After that mother and son were taken east to Buland Head, and Odd was hanged there. As he was kicking on the gallows, Arnkel said to him, 'It's your own mother who has brought you to this evil end. One thing is sure – it's a wicked mother you have.'

'Maybe he has a wicked mother,' said Katla, 'but I never wanted him to suffer like this. Now I want you all to suffer because of me, indeed I'm sure you will. But there's no point in denying it any longer, I'm the one responsible for Gunnlaug's mishap, and it's me that caused all the trouble. As for you, Arnkel, since your mother's dead, she can't bring you bad luck: but I lay this curse on you, that before this is over you'll suffer more because of your father than Odd has suffered because of me. The time will come when everyone will see what kind of a scoundrel your father is.'

They stoned Katla to death just below the cliffs, then went back to Mavahlid, stayed the night there, and rode home the following day. The news of what had happened soon spread, but no one felt sorry about it. So another winter passed.

❧

21. ARNKEL'S ADVICE

One day in the spring Arnkel sent for his kinsman, Thorarin, along with Vermund and Alfgeir, and asked what kind of help would be most welcome. Should they go to the assembly, and ask their friends for help?

'There seem to be two ways of looking at it,' he went on. 'If there's a settlement you'll have to pay out a great deal of money in compensation for those killed or wounded, though our presence in court may make matters worse, particularly if we press our case very strongly. The other course open is to do everything we can to help you go abroad with all your money, and take a chance on what becomes of the farm if we can't sell it.'

This was the kind of help Alfgeir thought best, and anyway Thorarin said he couldn't afford to pay compensation for all the offences he had committed. Vermund said he would stand by Thorarin whether he wanted Vermund to go abroad with him, or fight alongside him against his enemies in Iceland. Thorarin decided to accept Arnkel's offer to help him go abroad, so they sent a message west to Eyr telling Bjorn, the captain, to do all he could to ready the ship immediately.

☙

22. EXILE

Now we come back to Snorri the Priest, who had taken charge of the action over the killing of his brother-in-law Thorbjorn. He asked his sister Thurid to come and stay at Helgafell, as rumour had it that Bjorn Asbrandsson of Kamb was paying regular visits to Frodriver and carrying on with her. When Snorri heard that the ship was being made ready, he realized it must be Arnkel's plan to avoid paying compensation for the killings, since there had been no offer of a settlement.

All the same, things were quiet till Summons Days. Then Snorri gathered a force and rode eighty strong over to Alftafjord. It was the law in those days that the summons for manslaughter had to be made within earshot of the killers or wherever they lived, but neighbours were not cited as witnesses till the assembly was due.

When the men of Bolstad saw Snorri's party coming up, they began arguing about whether or not to fight, since there were a good many of them, but Arnkel was against it. 'Snorri's going to have his legal rights,' he said, and told them not to do anything that was unnecessary.

When Snorri got to Bolstad, nobody made any trouble. He summonsed Thorarin and all the others involved in the killings to the Thor's Ness Assembly. Arnkel listened closely. After that, Snorri and his men rode off to Ulfarsfell, and when they had gone, Thorarin made this verse:

> Not for desperate deeds
> have I, who's endured
> the fierce storms of the field,
> been denied fair play:
> my armed enemies
> would brand me outlaw:
> favour us, you gods,
> with the force to outface them.

That morning, Snorri the Priest rode across the ridge to Hrisar, over to Drapuhlid, west by Svinavatn to Hrauns Fjord, and from there by the normal route west to Trollahals, without breaking his journey till he came to Salteyrar Mouth, where some of his men laid hands on the Norwegian crew and others began burning the ship. When this was done, Snorri the Priest and his men rode back home.

When Arnkel heard that Snorri had burnt the ship, he boarded a boat with Vermund and several others and rowed north across the fjord over to Dogurdar Ness, where a Norwegian ship was beached. Arnkel and Vermund bought it, and Arnkel gave Thorarin his share, but Vermund kept the other half. They sailed the ship out to Dimun Island and fitted it out for the voyage. Arnkel stayed with them till they were ready to set off, then went with them as far as Ellida Island, where they parted the best of friends. Thorarin and Vermund sailed out to sea, and Arnkel went back to his farm. Everyone agreed that he had been more than generous with his help.

Snorri the Priest went to the Thor's Ness Assembly and pressed his charges. The outcome was that Thorarin and all those involved with him in the killings were sentenced to outlawry. After the Assembly, Snorri confiscated all of their property he could lay hands on, and that was the end of the lawsuit.

☯

23. INSULTS

As was said earlier, Vigfus, son of Bjorn Ottarsson, lived at Drapuhlid and married Thorgerd, Thorbeinir's-daughter. Vigfus was a good farmer, but a difficult man to get on with. He had a nephew called Bjorn staying with him, a loose-tongued, worthless sort of fellow.

In the autumn after the Mavahlid affair, Thorbjorn the Stout's herd of horses was found dead up in the mountains. His stallion had been driven from the pastures by Thorarin's and then the whole herd had been snowed under and killed.

That same autumn a crowd of people gathered at Tunga between the Lax Rivers south of Helga Fell to sort the sheep. Snorri sent some of his men there with his uncle Mar Hallvardsson in charge. Snorri had a shepherd called Helgi. Bjorn, Vigfus's nephew, was lying on top of the wall of the pen holding a shepherd's crook, while Helgi was sorting out the sheep. Bjorn asked him whose sheep he had just taken, and when they looked at it, they saw it had Vigfus's earmarks.

'You're not very particular about the sheep you're picking up today,' said Bjorn.

'It's even riskier for you,' said Helgi, 'living so close to common pasture.'

'What could a thief like you mean by that?' asked Bjorn. He jumped to his feet and lashed out at Helgi with the crook, knocking him senseless.

Mar saw what had happened, pulled out his sword, and lunged at Bjorn. The thrust caught him in the arm just below the shoulder, giving him a nasty wound. At that the sheep-sorters took sides, but some people stepped in and broke up the fighting, so for the present nothing happened.

Next morning Vigfus rode down to Helgafell and demanded compensation for the insult, but Snorri said he wasn't able to judge between the two incidents. Vigfus got angry, and they parted on cool terms.

In the spring Vigfus raised a court action over the wounding and put the case before the Thor's Ness Assembly, but Snorri made a counter-charge against Bjorn. Bjorn was found guilty of unlawful assault on Helgi, and got no compensation for the wound, even though he carried his arm in a sling after that.

24. EIRIK THE RED

At this Assembly Thorgest the Old and the sons of Thord Gellir brought an action against Eirik the Red for the killing of Thorgest's sons the autumn before, when Eirik went over to Breidabolstad to claim his bench-boards. It was a well-attended Assembly. Each side had kept a large standing force.

During the Assembly Eirik got his ship ready at Eirik's Bay on Oxna Island. He had the backing of Thorbjorn Vifilsson, Killer-Styr, the sons of Thorbrand of Alftafjord and Eyjolf Æsuson of Svin Island, but of all his supporters Styr was the only one who attended the Assembly. He persuaded all those he could to withdraw their support from Thorgest, and then pleaded with Snorri the Priest not to join Thorgest in the attack on Eirik after the Assembly. In return he promised to back Snorri any time he had trouble on his hands. Snorri accepted the offer and took no part in the quarrel.

After the Assembly, Thorgest and his men set out to the

islands in a number of boats, but Eyjolf Æsuson hid Eirik's ship in Dimun Bay, and that was where Styr and Thorbjorn came to join Eirik. Eyjolf and Styr did just as Arnkel had done and went with Eirik out beyond Ellida Island, each in his own boat.

It was on this voyage that Eirik the Red discovered Greenland. He stayed there for three years, and then went back to Iceland. The following year he set out to colonize Greenland, fourteen years before Christianity was adopted by law in Iceland.[1]

❦

25. THE SWEDISH BERSERKS

Now to come back to Vermund and Thorarin the Black, they made landfall in Norway north of Trondheim Fjord and sailed up to Trondheim. The ruler of Norway at the time was Earl Hakon Sigurdarson.[1] Vermund went to see him and became his retainer, but in the autumn Thorarin sailed west with Alfgeir to the British Isles and Vermund gave them his share in the ship. Now Thorarin is out of the story.

Earl Hakon was in residence at Lade that winter, and Vermund stayed with him there in great favour. The Earl knew that Vermund belonged to a distinguished family in Iceland, and that was why he treated him so well.

With the Earl were two Swedish brothers called Halli and Leiknir. They were by far the biggest and strongest men in Norway or anywhere else at that time. They used to go berserk, and once they had worked themselves up into a frenzy, they were wholly unlike human beings, storming

1. The events in this chapter, culminating in Eirik the Red's colonization of Greenland in 985 or 986, are described in more detail in *Eirik's Saga* and *Grœnlendinga Saga*. See *The Vinland Sagas*, (Penguin Classics, 1965).

1. Earl Hakon Sigurdarson was ruler of Norway 975–95.

about like mad dogs and afraid of neither fire nor weapons. Most of the time they were not hard to get on with as long as they were left in peace, but once anybody gave them the slightest offence, they became extremely violent. King Eirik the Victorious of Sweden[2] had given them to the Earl and warned him to look after them. The King told him nothing less than the truth, which was that the berserks were good men to have as allies as long as their tempers remained under control.

In the spring after Vermund had wintered with the Earl, he wanted to go back to Iceland and asked him for leave to sail. The Earl said he could go if he wished, but asked him to think about something first. 'Is there anything of mine you'd particularly like to have,' he said, 'a gift which would contribute to your prestige and do honour and credit to both of us?'

Vermund thought it over, wondering what he should ask for. Then it struck him how much it would strengthen his position in Iceland if he could have the berserks as his followers, so he decided to find out if the Earl would give him the berserks. Vermund had a good reason for wanting them. It seemed to him that his brother Styr was growing more than a match for him, for Styr kept bullying him, just as he bullied almost everyone else. With the berserks to back him up, Vermund did not think Styr would find it so easy to push him around.

So Vermund told the Earl he'd consider it an honour if he would give him the berserks to serve and protect him. 'It seems to me,' said the Earl, 'that you've asked for the one thing that will be of no use to you even if I grant it. I know you'll find the berserks troublesome and arrogant if you don't get on with them. As I see it, controlling those ruffians and keeping them in their place is going to be far too much for a mere farmer's son, even though they've been quiet enough in my service.'

Vermund said he was ready to risk it if the Earl would agree to give them to him. The Earl told him to find out first from the

2. King Eirik ruled Sweden from c.950 to c.993.

berserks themselves whether they would go with him, and Vermund did so, asking if they would be his men and come with him to Iceland. In return he promised to treat them well and give them anything they wanted when they asked for it. The berserks said they had never thought of going to Iceland, since from what they'd heard, there was no chieftain there worthy of their service.

'But since you're so keen to take us with you to Iceland, Vermund,' they said, 'we want you to know this, that if ever you refuse us anything which we want and you have the power to give, we won't be at all pleased.'

Vermund said it would never come to that, and got their promise to come with him to Iceland, provided the Earl gave his approval. Vermund went to see the Earl to tell him what had happened, and the Earl decided the berserks should go with him to Iceland, 'since you think it'll do so much for your prestige'. But he gave a warning that he would take it as a personal affront if Vermund were to treat them badly once they became his men. Vermund said there was no reason to think it would ever come to that, then set off to Iceland with the berserks aboard. He had a good passage and reached home the same summer that Eirik the Red sailed to Greenland, as we have described.

Soon after Vermund came home, the berserk Halli said he wanted Vermund to find him a suitable wife, but Vermund knew of no respectable woman who wanted to be landed with a berserk for the rest of her life, so he kept putting him off. When Halli saw what was happening, he became aggressive and ill-tempered, and this led to a bitter quarrel between them. The berserks kept swaggering about, threatening Vermund, and he began to regret ever having taken them in.

In the autumn Vermund held a great feast and invited his brother Styr, Arnkel the Priest, and the Men of Eyr. After the feast Vermund offered Arnkel the berserks and said they might come in very useful, but Arnkel refused the gift. Then Vermund asked Arnkel for advice about how to get out of his difficulty, and Arnkel suggested giving the berserks to Styr. 'He's so arrogant and unjust himself,' said Arnkel, 'that most likely he'll be able to cope with them.'

So when Styr was ready to go, Vermund came up and spoke to him. 'Brother,' he said, 'I'd like to put an end to the coolness between us since before I went abroad. We ought to remember our kinship and stay good friends. I'd like to give you these two warriors I brought from Norway, to serve and protect you. With followers like these to back you up I don't think anyone would have the power to stand up to you.'

'I'd very much like us to be on friendlier terms, brother,' said Styr, 'but from what I've heard about these men you brought to Iceland, they'd be a liability rather than an asset, and won't bring anyone much luck. I'm certainly not having them in my house. I'm unpopular enough as it is, without their adding to my troubles.'

'What advice would you give me, then, brother, to get me out of this?' asked Vermund.

'That's a different matter entirely,' said Styr. 'To help you out of your troubles is one thing, getting these men as a gift from you is quite another. I'm not having them on any account. Still, now we're friends again, I suppose there's no one more duty-bound to help you out than I am.'

Yet in spite of Styr's refusal, Vermund still persuaded him to take the berserks. The brothers parted the best of friends, and Styr went back home taking the berserks with him. At first they refused to go and said Vermund had no right to sell them or give them away as if they were slaves, but in the end they had to admit it would suit them better to serve Styr than Vermund.

At first, the berserks and Styr got on well together. They both went with him on his trip across the bay when he killed Thorbjorn Kjalki of Kjalkafjord. Thorbjorn had a bed-closet built with thick beams, but the berserks forced the joints apart, and they were able to break into it without any trouble at all, though it was Styr himself who killed Thorbjorn Kjalki.

❦

26. ATTEMPT ON SNORRI'S LIFE

One day in autumn after the berserks had come to stay with
Styr, Vigfus of Drapuhlid set out with three slaves to make
charcoal at a place called Seljabrekkur. One of the slaves was
called Svart the Strong. As they were going through the wood,
Vigfus said, 'It's a sad thing, Svart, when a good strong fellow
like you isn't a free man. You must take it badly.'

'I take it hard,' said Svart, 'but there's nothing I can do about
it.'

'What would you do for me if I gave you your freedom?'
asked Vigfus.

'I haven't any money so I can't buy my freedom,' said Svart,
'but if there's something I can do to win it, then I'm ready for
anything.'

'Go over to Helgafell and kill Snorri the Priest,' said Vigfus,
'and once you've done that, you can have your freedom and
plenty more besides.'

'I'll never manage it,' said Svart.

'I'll tell you how to go about it,' said Vigfus. 'I guarantee
there won't be any risk to your life.'

'Tell me more,' said Svart.

'Go over to Helgafell and into the loft above the main door.
Then pull up a plank or two from the floor so that you can push
your halberd through the gap, and when Snorri goes out to the
privy, drive the halberd hard down into his back so that the
blade goes right through his body. Then climb on to the roof,
jump down from the wall, and get away under cover of
darkness.'

With these instructions in mind Svart set off over to Helgafell. He broke a hole in the ceiling above the main door and
scrambled into the loft. While all this was going on, Snorri and
his men were sitting by the fire. In those days every farm had

an outside privy. When Snorri and his men got up from the fire to go out, he was ahead of the rest, and by the time Svart made his thrust, Snorri was already through the door. Mar Hallvard-sson came close on Snorri's heels, and it was he who took Svart's blow. The blade caught him in the shoulder and sliced across the arm, but it wasn't a serious wound. Svart scrambled out on to the roof, but as he jumped down from the wall, he slipped on the pavement. It was a nasty fall, and Snorri had him before he could get back onto his feet. Once they began questioning him, he told them not only all that had passed between Vigfus and himself, but also where Vigfus was, making charcoal at Seljabrekkur.

When Mar's wound had been seen to, Snorri set out over to Drapuhlid with six men. As they made their way up the hillside they could see the fire where Vigfus and his slaves were making the charcoal. They took them by surprise and put Vigfus to death, but spared his slaves. After that Snorri went home, but sent the slaves back to Drapuhlid to tell people the news. Next morning a burial mound was raised over Vigfus, and that same day his widow Thorgerd went over to Bolstad to tell her uncle Arnkel about it. She asked him to take action over the killing, but he refused and said, that was the business of the Kjalleklings, who were Vigfus's kinsmen. He proposed Styr as the one more suited to raise the action, since he was always meddling in everything.

Thormod Trefilsson made this verse about the killing of Vigfus:

> The war-chief Snorri
> struck down and slew
> the first of his victims
> when he vanquished Vigfus,
> and left his corpse
> as carrion, for crows
> to gorge their greed
> on gobbets of his flesh.

❦

27. THORGERD GETS HELP

Thorgerd went over to Hraun and asked Styr to take action over the killing of his kinsman Vigfus.

'Last spring, when Snorri the Priest kept out of our quarrel with the Thorgestlings,' said Styr, 'I promised I'd never act against him in any lawsuit where there were plenty of others just as much involved as myself. You'd better ask my brother Vermund to take up the case, or some other member of our family.'

So Thorgerd made a trip out to Bjorn's Haven and asked Vermund for help. She said it was really his business.

'Vigfus trusted you before any of his kinsmen,' she said.

'I agree it's my duty to help you with the case,' said Vermund. 'I'm not going to shoulder my kinsmen's burden, but I'll do all I can for you in the way of advice and support. First, I want you to go over to Eyr and see Steinthor, Vigfus's kinsman. He's always spoiling for a fight, and it's about time he tried his hand at a lawsuit.'

'You're all putting me to a lot of trouble,' said Thorgerd, 'but I won't hold back if I can get results.'

Next she went over to Eyr to see Steinthor and asked him to take over the action for manslaughter.

'Why come to me for help?' asked Steinthor. 'I'm only a young man, and I've never taken part in a lawsuit before. Vigfus had plenty of closer kinsmen than me and a lot more pushing, so I can hardly be expected to take this case off their hands. But naturally, if my kinsmen decide to take action over the killing, I won't let them down.'

And that was all the answer Thorgerd could get from him. So she travelled to the other side of the fjord to see Vermund, told him what had happened, and said it would be the end of her lawsuit if he refused to take charge.

'If it's any consolation to you,' said Vermund, 'there's still a good chance that action will be taken. Promise to follow my advice, and I'll tell you what to do.'

'I'd do almost anything to help,' she said.

'All right,' said Vermund, 'go back and have your husband's body dug up, then take his head to Arnkel. Tell him this head wouldn't have left the action to others if Arnkel had needed it.'

Thorgerd said she failed to see how that was going to help. As far as she could tell, everybody seemed only too keen to add to her trouble and misery. 'But I'll do as you suggest,' she said. 'I can only hope it'll make my enemies suffer.'

So she went back home and did just as she had been told. When she came to Bolstad, she told Arnkel that her husband's kinsmen wanted him to take charge of the manslaughter action over Vigfus and that they had promised to back him up. When Arnkel said he had already told her what he thought of the case, she pulled the head from under her cloak.

'Here's a head,' she said, 'that would never have shirked action if you'd been killed and its help had been needed.'

Arnkel was horrified and pushed her away.

'Get out of here,' he said, 'tell Vigfus's kinsmen they'd better be just as determined to back me against Snorri the Priest as I'll be in pressing charges. I don't know how this case will turn out, though I'll surely be the last man to give up. Obviously Vermund gave you this advice, but if he and I are fighting the same battle, it won't be me he'll have to goad into action.'

With that Thorgerd went back home.

The winter passed and in the spring Arnkel started a manslaughter action against all who had taken part in the attack on Vigfus, with the exception of Snorri the Priest. But Snorri brought a counter-action for attempted manslaughter on his own behalf, and another action for the wounding of Mar, claiming that Vigfus had been lawfully killed. Both sides came to the Thor's Ness Assembly with a large following, but all the Kjalleklings supported Arnkel, and they had the stronger force. Arnkel pleaded the case forcefully, but when judgement was about to be passed, peacemakers intervened, and thanks to their plea the whole issue was referred to arbitration. Snorri agreed to accept the verdict of the arbitrators. For the killing of Vigfus he was made to pay a large fine, and Mar was to stay abroad for three years. Snorri paid his fine on the spot, and when the Assembly broke up, every lawsuit had been settled peacefully.

☙

28. THE END OF THE BERSERKS

Now we take up the story where we left off.

The berserks had not been long in Styr's service, when Halli took a fancy to Styr's-daughter Asdis. She was a good-looking young woman, but very proud and self-assured. When Styr found out they had been talking together, he told Halli not to bring shame and disgrace on him by trying to seduce his daughter.

'I've said nothing to your daughter for you to be ashamed of,' said Halli. 'I'm not just doing it to make trouble, and I might as well tell you straight out that I'm so much in love with her I can't put her out of my mind. I want you and me to be close friends. Let me marry your daughter Asdis, and in return I'll give you my word and swear to be your loyal friend. The backing you'll get from my brother Leiknir and me will be stronger than any two men will ever give in all Iceland. Our support will do more to raise your status here than if you were to marry off your daughter to the greatest farmer in Breida-fjord, and that should make up for my lack of money. But if you decide to turn me down, it'll be the end of our friendship, and then each of us will just have to take what's coming to him. In any case there's not much you can do to stop me talking with Asdis.'

Halli having spoken his piece, Styr was very quiet, not

knowing what to say. After a while he asked, 'Is this a serious proposal, or are you just playing about and trying to start an argument?'

'Whatever your answer,' said Halli, 'get one thing clear, I'm not doing this for a joke. Our whole friendship depends on what you have to say about it.'

'Before I can give you an answer, I'll have to ask my friends about it,' said Styr.

'I give you three days to talk it over with anyone you like,' said Halli, 'but you're not putting me off any longer than that, for I'm not the kind of suitor who cares to be kept waiting.'

With that they parted. Next morning Styr rode over to Helgafell and saw Snorri, who asked him to stay. Styr said he only wanted to have a word and then ride back home. Snorri asked if it was something serious he wanted to discuss.

'I'd call it that,' said Styr.

'Then we'd better go to the top of Helga Fell,' said Snorri. 'Plans made there have never been known to fail.'

'As you wish,' said Styr.

They went to the top of the hill and sat there in conversation till evening, but nobody knew what they were talking about. After that Styr rode back home.

Next morning Styr took Halli aside. Halli asked what he was doing about the proposal.

'Everybody thinks you're far too badly off,' said Styr. 'Are you willing to compensate for your poverty?'

'I'll do whatever I can,' said Halli, 'but it can't be to lay out money, as I haven't got any.'

'I can see you'd be offended if I refused to let you marry my daughter,' said Styr, 'so I'm going to do as people used to in the old days. Before you win her hand, I'll set you a few difficult tasks.'

'What do you have in mind?' asked Halli.

'Clear a path right across the lava-field, all the way to Bjorn's Haven,' said Styr, 'then set up a dyke across the lava to mark the boundary-line between the two farms, and last of all build a sheep-shed on my side of the dyke. Once you've managed all that, you can have my daughter for your wife.'

'I'm not used to hard work,' said Halli, 'but I'll agree to anything that helps smooth the bridal path.'

So Styr said they'd arrange terms.

The berserks set to work clearing the path, a really massive undertaking. Next they set up the dyke, traces of which can still be seen, then when they finished the dyke, they started on the sheep-shed. While they were working away, Styr had a bath-house built on his farm at Hraun. It was partly below ground level, and immediately above the fireplace there was a skylight for pouring water through from the outside. This bath-house was really hot.

When the two berserks had nearly finished their allotted tasks and on the very last day were busy at the sheep-shed, Styr's-daughter Asdis went out for a walk near the farmhouse wearing her finest clothes and came quite close to them. Halli and his brother spoke to her, but she took no notice. Then Halli made this verse:

> Tell me, my gold-adorned
> girl-friend so graceful,
> where do you walk
> in your elegant way?
> Through the whole winter
> not once have I watched you
> wandering by
> in such wonderful wear.

Leiknir said:

> So high has no lady
> e'er held her head,
> gold-adorned,
> as this delicate damsel:
> What's the deep mystery
> masked by your manner?
> In your sweet voice, smoothly
> sing out your secret.

But she walked away from them. That evening the berserks came home, completely worn out. What happens to those who go berserk is that once the rage leaves them, they seem to lose all their strength. Styr came out to welcome them and thanked them for what they had done. He invited them to take a bath before having a rest. This they did, but as soon as they were inside the bath-house, Styr sealed it off, heaping stones on top of the trapdoor leading up from the bath. In front of it he spread a wet ox-hide, then had a lot of water poured in through the skylight above the hearth, which made the room so terribly hot that the berserks found it unbearable and began attacking the door. Halli managed to smash through and scramble outside, but he slipped on the ox-hide, and Styr gave him his death-wound. When Leiknir came rushing through the door, Styr drove a spear through him, and he fell back dead into the bath-house. Then Styr had the bodies laid out for burial and taken over to the lava-field. There they were buried in a lava-pit so deep that nothing could be seen from the bottom except the blue sky above. This place lies close to the path.

At the berserks' burial, Styr made this verse:

> I knew that these berserks,
> unbending in battle,
> would prove a fierce pair
> to me and my friends.
> But I'm not afraid
> of the fury of the fight:
> I've buried those berserks'
> bodies in a pit!

When Snorri heard the news, he rode off to Hraun, where he and Styr spent the whole day talking together. Afterwards they announced that Asdis, Styr's-daughter, was to marry Snorri the Priest. The wedding took place in the autumn, and everyone agreed that both men had strengthened their positions by these family ties. Snorri was the shrewder of the two and a better counsellor, but Styr was more the man of action, and neither was short of kinsmen, or other support in the district.

☙

29. A LOVE AFFAIR

There was a man called Thorodd whose family belonged to Medalfell Strand. People trusted him. He was a great sea-going trader and had his own ship. Thorodd went on an Irish trading-trip to Dublin, just after Earl Sigurd Hlodvesson of Orkney had been raiding in the Hebrides and the Isle of Man.[1] The Earl forced the people of Man to pay him tribute, and once agreement had been reached, he sailed back to Orkney, leaving his agents to collect the tax, which was to be paid in refined silver. When they had gathered the money and all was ready, they sailed off before a south-westerly wind, but shortly after that it began to blow south-easterly, then easterly. Soon a strong gale blew up, and they were driven north of Ireland, where the ship was wrecked on an uninhabited island.

That is where Thorodd of Iceland found them on his way back from Dublin. The Earl's men shouted for help, so Thorodd had a boat lowered and jumped in himself. When he reached them, they pleaded with him to save them and offered him money if he would take them back to Earl Sigurd in Orkney, but Thorodd felt it could not be done as he was all set for Iceland. Still they kept pressing him, for they were convinced that their very lives and property were at stake and that the people of Ireland and the Hebrides where they had been

1. See *Orkneyingasaga* (Penguin Classics, 1981), Chapter 11.

raiding could easily make slaves of them, so in the end Thorodd agreed to sell them his tow-boat for a large part of the tribute. The Earl's men sailed the boat to Orkney, and Thorodd went on his way without a lifeboat. He made landfall in the south, then sailed west into Breida Fjord, putting in safely at Dogurdar Ness. After that, people started calling him Thorodd the Tribute-Trader.

In the autumn, shortly after the killing of Thorbjorn the Stout, he went to Helgafell to stay with Snorri the Priest. Thorbjorn's widow Thurid, who was Snorri the Priest's sister, was also spending the winter at Helgafell. Thorodd had been there only a short while when he asked Snorri for his sister's hand. Snorri knew Thorodd was quite well-off and a decent man too, so seeing that Thurid needed someone to take care of her, it seemed a good idea from every point of view that he should marry his sister to Thorodd. Snorri himself held the wedding-feast at Helgafell later that winter. In the spring Thorodd took over the farm at Frodriver and became a good and thrifty farmer.

No sooner had Thurid settled down at Frodriver than Bjorn Asbrandsson started calling on her, and soon the rumour got about that he was carrying on with her. Thorodd warned him off, but it made no difference.

At that time Thorir Wood-Leg was farming at Arnarhvall. His sons, Orn and Val, had grown into fine, promising men. They were critical of Thorodd for putting up with the disgrace Bjorn was causing him, and offered their support should Thorodd decide to put a stop to Bjorn's visits.

One day Bjorn came to Frodriver and settled down for a talk with Thurid. Thorodd used to stay sitting in the room until Bjorn left, but this time he was nowhere to be seen.

'Watch your step when you go back home, Bjorn,' said Thurid. 'I've a feeling Thorodd would like to make this visit your last. I think there'll be people lying in wait for you on your way home, and Thorodd will see to it the odds aren't fair when you meet.'

Then Bjorn made this verse:

> From fair golden daybreak
> to deep blue darkness,
> long should the day have lasted,
> my delight, my despair!
> As the day is dying
> a drink I'll pledge
> to the pain-filled memory
> of passing pleasures.

Bjorn took his weapons and set out for home. Suddenly, as he was coming up by Digramull, five men sprang up in front of him, Thorodd with two of his farm-hands and the sons of Thorir Wood-Leg. They set upon Bjorn, but he defended himself with skill and courage. The Thorissons attacked him fiercely and got in several blows, but he killed them both. Then Thorodd and his servants ran off, Thorodd only slightly wounded, and the servants not at all. Bjorn made his way home. He went into the living-room, and his mother told a servant-maid to see to him. When she came back into the room with a light, she saw he had blood all over him, so she went to tell Asbrand, his father, that Bjorn had come home soaked in blood. Asbrand came into the room and asked Bjorn why he was bleeding so badly. 'Did you happen to run into Thorodd?' he asked. Bjorn told him he had. When Asbrand asked him what had happened between them, Bjorn said:

> Sword-skilled, I slaughtered
> the sons of Wood-Leg.
> It was harder for Thorodd
> to thrust me through,
> than to lie making love
> to his elegant lady
> or rob the Earl's traders
> and take their taxes.

After that Asbrand dressed his wounds, and they healed completely.

Thorodd asked Snorri to support him in the action over the killing of the Thorissons, and Snorri took up his case at the Thor's Ness Assembly. The sons of Thorlak of Eyr supported Bjorn's side. The outcome was that Asbrand shook hands, gave pledges on behalf of his son Bjorn, and paid the fine for the killings, but Bjorn was outlawed and banished from Iceland for three years. He went abroad the same summer.

That was the summer Thurid of Frodriver gave birth to a boy, who was named Kjartan. He was brought up at Frodriver and soon grew to be a big promising lad.

Bjorn sailed to Norway, then south to Denmark, and from there he travelled on east to Jomsborg. At that time Palna-Toki was the leader of the Jomsvikings.[2] Bjorn joined the vikings and they thought highly of him as a fighting man. He was at Jomsborg when Styrbjorn the Strong conquered it, and afterwards went to Sweden when the Jomsvikings were fighting on Styrbjorn's side. He took part in the Battle of Fyrisvellir at which Styrbjorn was killed, but Bjorn and a number of other Jomsvikings made their escape into a forest. As long as Palna-Toki lived, Bjorn stayed with him. People considered Bjorn a great warrior and the bravest of men in any dangerous situation.

❧

30. THOROLF TWIST-FOOT

Now we come back to Thorolf Twist-Foot, who was getting very old. The older he got, the more violent he grew, and there was increasing bad-blood between him and his son Arnkel.

One day Thorolf rode over to Ulfarsfell to see Ulfar, a

2. The Jomsvikings were a band of marauders who had their base near the mouth of the River Oder on the Baltic. Their adventures are described in the semi-legendary *Jomsvikings' Saga*, but they are also mentioned in the *Heimskringla* and elsewhere in saga literature. The leaders of the Jomsvikings are said to have been killed in the Battle of Liavag in 994.

hard-working farmer who was known to be better at gathering in his hay than anyone else. Ulfar was so lucky with his livestock that none of his beasts ever perished from starvation or blizzards. When Thorolf met Ulfar he asked him how he should organize work on the farm, and whether he thought the summer would be good for drying the hay.

'The best I can do for you,' said Ulfar, 'is tell you how I'll go about things myself. I'm having the scythes taken out today and then we'll mow all the hay we can till the end of the week, as I think there's going to be a heavy rainfall. After that there should be a good drying spell for a fortnight.'

He could forecast the weather more accurately than anyone else, so it turned out exactly as he had predicted.

Thorolf went back home. He had several farm-hands and ordered them to start the haymaking at once. The weather turned out just as Ulfar had said. Thorolf and Ulfar had joint ownership of a meadow up on the ridge, both had a lot of hay there, which they were drying and gathering into large stacks. Early one morning when Thorolf got up, it was so cloudy he thought there would be no drying-weather that day, so he told his slaves to prepare for stacking the hay. He said they were to work at it all day and do the best they could. 'The weather seems very unsettled,' he said. The slaves got dressed and set to work, with Thorolf stacking the hay, pressing them to work harder and finish the job.

Ulfar got up early that morning to take a look round, and when he came back inside, the farm-hands asked what the weather was like. He told them to go back to sleep. 'The weather's fine,' he said, 'it'll clear up. Today I want you to mow the home meadow, and then we'll gather in the hay on the ridge tomorrow.' The weather turned out just as he said it would, and in the evening he sent one of his farm-hands up to the ridge to take a look at his haystacks there. During the day Thorolf used three yoke of oxen to cart the hay, and by the early afternoon it had all been brought in. Then he told his slaves to fetch Ulfar's hay as well, and they did exactly as he told them. When Ulfar's servant saw what they were doing, he ran back home with the news. Ulfar was furious and rushed up to the ridge to ask Thorolf why he was robbing him. Thorolf said he didn't care what Ulfar had to say. He kept rattling on and grew so violent they came close to fighting. Ulfar saw the best thing he could do was to leave, so he went to see Arnkel, told him about his loss and asked for his help, since without that there was nothing he could do. Arnkel promised to ask his father to pay damages for the hay, though he thought it very unlikely that it would make the least difference.

Arnkel went to see his father and said he ought to pay Ulfar for the hay he had taken, but Thorolf replied that for a slave Ulfar was already far too well-off. Then Arnkel asked him as a personal favour to pay compensation for the hay. Thorolf said he would do nothing of the sort, though he might do something to make matters worse for Ulfar. With that they parted.

Arnkel went back to Ulfar and told him what Thorolf had said. Ulfar thought Arnkel could have been much firmer, and said he ought to be able to make his father do as he wanted. Arnkel paid Ulfar's price for the hay, and next time he saw his father, Arnkel asked him for the money, but Thorolf gave the same bad-tempered answer as before, and they parted on angry terms. In the autumn Arnkel had seven of Thorolf's oxen taken from the mountain pasture and slaughtered for the table. Thorolf was furious and demanded payment for the oxen, but Arnkel said it was just to cover the cost of the hay taken from Ulfar. This infuriated Thorolf even more. He said Ulfar was the cause of all the trouble and threatened to make him pay dearly for it.

ॐ

31. ARSON

That winter, about Christmas time, Thorolf held a great feast and gave his slaves plenty to drink. When he had got them drunk, he talked them into going to Ulfarsfell, where they were to set fire to the house and burn Ulfar to death inside. As a reward he promised to free them. The slaves said they would do it for the sake of their freedom, and trust him to keep his word. Six of them set out across to Ulfarsfell, where they got hold of some firewood, piled it up against the house, and set fire to it.

Over at Bolstad, Arnkel was drinking with his men, and as they were going to bed they saw the fire at Ulfarsfell. They rushed over, seized the slaves, and put out the fire. The house was only slightly damaged. In the morning Arnkel had the slaves taken out to Vadilshofdi and hanged.

After that Ulfar formally made over his property to Arnkel, who then became his legal guardian. This contract didn't please the Thorbrandssons at all, for they thought that since Ulfar was their freedman, they had a claim to his property. This led to so much bitter feeling between them they could no longer even hold common games though they had always done so before. Arnkel was the strongest competitor of them all, and there was only one man who could rival him, Freystein Bofi, Thorbrand's foster-son, the next best competitor there. Most people thought Freystein was really Thorbrand's own son, but his mother was a slave-girl. He was a handsome man and very strong.

Thorolf Twist-Foot was far from pleased about Arnkel killing his slaves and demanded compensation, but Arnkel refused to pay a penny, and this made Thorolf even worse tempered.

One day Thorolf rode out to Helgafell to see Snorri the Priest. Snorri offered him hospitality, but Thorolf said he was in no need of food. 'I'm here because I want you to help me get justice,' he said. 'I think you're the leading farmer in the district, and it's up to you to set right any wrongs people have suffered around here.'

'Who's been treading on your rights?' asked Snorri.

'My son Arnkel,' said Thorolf.

'You shouldn't complain,' said Snorri. 'You ought always to be on Arnkel's side, he's a much better man than you.'

'That's not true,' said Thorolf. 'Arnkel bullies me more than ever. If you would take action about the killing of the slaves, Snorri, and prosecute Arnkel for it, I'd be a good friend to you. I wouldn't claim more than a part of the compensation for myself.'

'I don't want to get caught up in a quarrel between you and your son,' said Snorri.

'You're no friend of Arnkel's either,' said Thorolf, 'and though you think me a miser, I shan't be so stingy this time. I know you'd like to own Kraka Ness with all that woodland, the best in the whole district, and I'll hand it all over to you formally on condition you start proceedings over the killing of my slaves. I want you to press your case so hard, your reputation will be greater than ever. Those who wronged me must be put in their place. No matter how closely they may be related to me, show mercy to none of them.'

Snorri thought it over and, so the story goes, he wanted the woodland so badly that he formally accepted ownership of the land and promised to raise a court action over the killing of the slaves. Thorolf rode back home very pleased with himself, but most people had their doubts about this arrangement.

In the spring Snorri brought an action against Arnkel for the killing of the slaves and referred the case to the Thor's Ness Assembly. Both sides turned up at the Assembly in large numbers. Snorri pleaded the case, but when it came to court Arnkel asked the court to dismiss it on the ground that the slaves were committing arson when they were caught. Snorri agreed that the slaves could have been lawfully killed at the place where they committed the crime. 'But you took them over to Vadilshofdi to put them to death,' he said, 'and that's why compensation must be paid for them.'

In this way Snorri saved his case, and Arnkel's plea for dismissal was invalidated. Then people stepped in to reconcile them, and a settlement was made. Styr and his brother Vermund were chosen to arbitrate, and they awarded twelve ounces of silver for each slave, the entire amount to be paid on the spot at the Assembly. When the fine had been paid, Snorri handed it all over to Thorolf, who took it and said: 'It never occurred to me when I gave you my land that you'd be so slack in following this up. I'm sure that if I'd left it to Arnkel, he'd never have treated me so badly, or paid me such poor compensation for my slaves.'

'I don't see that the outcome discredits you in any way,' said Snorri, 'and as for your malice and injustice, I'm not staking my good name on it.'

'Don't worry, I'll never come to you again with my problems,' said Thorolf, 'and this trouble won't be the last to keep the neighbourhood awake.'

After that people went home from the Assembly, and if Arnkel and Snorri were unhappy about the outcome of the case, Thorolf was even more so.

☙

32. ULFAR IS KILLED

The story goes that Orlyg of Orlygsstad fell ill, and as he grew weaker, his brother Ulfar came to sit at his bedside. Orlyg died of this illness. As soon as he was dead, Ulfar sent for Arnkel, who hurried over to Orlygsstad, and he and Ulfar took charge of the entire property there.

When the Thorbrandssons heard of Orlyg's death, they went to Orlygsstad and laid claim to the property on the grounds that everything formerly belonging to their freedman was theirs. On the other hand, Ulfar argued that he was his brother's legal heir.

The Thorbrandssons asked Arnkel what he was going to do about it. He said that while Ulfar remained his partner, he wasn't going to let anyone rob him if he could help it. At that the Thorbrandssons went over to Helgafell to see Snorri the Priest. They asked him for help, but he said he had no intention of quarrelling with Arnkel over this, since they had been so slack as to let Arnkel and Ulfar be the first to lay hands on the property. The Thorbrandssons said that Snorri would be unable to cope with bigger issues, if he paid no attention to this one.

In the autumn Arnkel held a great feast. On such occasions, he would invite his friend Ulfar and always gave him parting gifts when he left. On the last day of the feast at Bolstad, Thorolf Twist-Foot set off on a journey to see his friend Spa-Gils, who was living at Spagilsstad in Thorsardale, and asked him to ride with him up to Ulfarsfell Ridge. Thorolf had a slave with him. Once they were up on the ridge, Thorolf said, 'That must be Ulfar there, on his way back from the feast, loaded with fine gifts. Spa-Gils, I want you to go and ambush him at the dyke at Ulfarsfell, I want you to kill him. In return I'll give you three ounces of silver and on top of that pay compensation for the killing; and when you've killed Ulfar you can relieve him of the fine gifts he got from Arnkel, then quickly make your way west from Ulfarsfell over to Kraka Ness. If anybody starts chasing after you, there's plenty of woodland for you to hide in. After that come back to me, and I'll see you come to no harm.'

Spa-Gils had a large family to support and badly needed the money, so he swallowed the bait. He went down to the dyke of the home meadow at Ulfarsfell, and it wasn't long before he saw Ulfar coming up from Bolstad, carrying a fine shield that Arnkel had given him and an ornamented sword. When they met, Spa-Gils asked if he could take a look at the sword, then started saying what a great fellow Ulfar was, and how he deserved to get such splendid gifts from prominent people. Ulfar began twirling his beard. But as soon as he handed over the sword and shield, Spa-Gils took the sword, ran Ulfar through with it, and set off from Ulfarsfell as fast as his legs would carry him in the direction of Kraka Ness.

Arnkel was standing outside when he saw this man running along, carrying a shield he thought he recognized. It seemed to him unlikely that Ulfar would ever have willingly surrendered the shield, so he told some of his people to go after the man.

'I think I see my father's hand in this,' said Arnkel, 'and since this man has probably already killed Ulfar, you'd better kill him right away, whoever he is. I don't want to see him.'

Arnkel himself took some men up to Ulfarsfell, and there they found Ulfar's body.

Thorolf Twist-Foot had been watching Spa-Gils as he ran west below Ulfar's Fell with the shield, and guessed what must have happened when he met Ulfar, so he turned to the slave he had with him. 'Go east to Karsstad,' he said to him, 'and tell the Thorbrandssons to hurry over to Ulfarsfell. Now that Ulfar's been killed, they'd better see to it they aren't robbed a second time of their freedman's inheritance.' After that Thorolf rode home, well pleased with a good day's work.

The men chasing after Spa-Gils caught up with him at a cliff that rises above the foreshore, and dragged the whole story out of him. After he had told them everything, they killed him and buried his body below the cliff. The sword and shield they took and gave back to Arnkel.

Thorolf's slave came to Karsstad and gave the Thorbrandssons his message. They set out at once for Ulfarsfell, but by the time they arrived Arnkel was already there with a number of men. The Thorbrandssons laid formal claim to Ulfar's property, but Arnkel presented the testimony of witnesses who had been there when Ulfar assigned his possessions to him. Arnkel said he planned to stand firm on his right to the property, since the original agreement had never been lawfully challenged. He warned them not to make any further claims, for he meant to treat the property just as if it were a part of his own inheritance.

The Thorbrandssons saw that they had no choice but to leave so once again they went to Helgafell to tell Snorri what had happened and ask for his help. Snorri said not for the first time had they been one move behind Arnkel.

'You'll never get the property from him now that he's got his hands on everything,' said Snorri. 'It's true the farm lies just as close to you, but the stronger is sure to win. Obviously Arnkel's going to get the best of it this time, as he always does in his dealings with you. It's a true saying, that what happens to others can happen to you. Arnkel tramples on everybody's rights in this neighbourhood, and will do as long as he lives, no matter how long or short his life may be.'

Thorleif Kimbi answered him. 'That's true enough, Snorri,' he said, 'you've every excuse for not wanting to defend our rights against Arnkel. In every quarrel with him you've been the loser, no matter what the issue.'

The Thorbrandssons went back home in an angry mood.

✿

33. THOROLF TWIST-FOOT DIES

Snorri the Priest started making use of Krakaness Wood and felled a good many trees there. Thorolf Twist-Foot thought he was ruining the wood and rode down to Helgafell to ask Snorri for the wood back, claiming that he had only leased it to Snorri, not given it away. Snorri said the matter could easily be settled, since all they needed was to ask the people who had witnessed their agreement; but unless their testimony went against him, he would refuse to hand over the woodland.

At that Thorolf went off in a rage. He rode east to Bolstad to see his son Arnkel, who gave his father a good welcome and asked why he had come.

'I've come to see you because I'm unhappy we're not getting on so well together,' said Thorolf. 'I'd like us to set things right, and be friends again as we ought. It's wrong for us to be feuding like this. It seems to me the two of us could be the top men in the district, what with your courage and my cunning.'

'I'd be a lot happier myself if we were on better terms,' said Arnkel.

'This is what I'd like us to do,' said Thorolf. 'Let's start our new friendship and confirm our reconciliation by claiming Krakaness Wood from Snorri the Priest. There's nothing I hate more than the way he lords it over us, and now he won't give me back the ownership of that woodland. He even claims I gave it to him as a present, and that's a downright lie.'

'It wasn't out of friendship towards me that you gave Snorri the wood,' said Arnkel, 'and I'm not going to let your malicious tongue talk me into fighting him over it. I know well enough that he has no legal right to it, but I won't have you and your ugly disposition gloating over any quarrel between me and Snorri.'

'I can think of another reason,' said Thorolf. 'It's your cowardly heart that's to blame, not the pleasure, which you grudge me, of seeing you two fight it out.'

'Think whatever you like,' said Arnkel, 'I'm starting no quarrel with Snorri over this woodland.'

With that they parted. Thorolf went back home in a rage, for he could see how difficult it was going to be for him to get what he wanted. It was evening when he reached home, and he sat down on the high-seat without uttering a word to anybody. He ate nothing all evening and stayed in his seat when the rest of the household went to bed. In the morning, when they got up Thorolf was still sitting there, dead.

Thorolf's widow sent someone to Arnkel to tell him his father had died, so Arnkel rode over to Hvamm with some of his servants. When they got there, his father was still sitting on the high-seat, and Arnkel went to make sure he was really dead. Everyone in the house was numb with terror, his death was so gruesome. When Arnkel went into the living-room he crossed the hall to get behind Thorolf, warning people to take care not to pass in front of the corpse until the eyes had been closed. He took Thorolf by the shoulders but had to use all his strength before he could force him down. After that he wrapped some clothes around Thorolf's head and got him ready for burial according to the custom of the time. He had a hole broken through the wall behind Thorolf, and the corpse was dragged outside. After a yoke of oxen had been hitched to a sled, Arnkel laid Thorolf on it, and they began driving it up through Thorsardale. It was hard work hauling Thorolf to his burial-place. When they got him there, they built a solid cairn over him.

After that Arnkel went back to Hvamm and took over all his father's possessions. He stayed for three days, and while he was there, nothing unusual happened. Then he went back home.

34. THOROLF'S GHOST

After Thorolf died, a good many people found it more and more unpleasant to stay out of doors once the sun had begun to go down. As the summer wore on, it became clear that Thorolf wasn't lying quiet, for after sunset no one out of doors was left in peace. There was another thing, too: the oxen which had been used to haul Thorolf's body were ridden to death by demons, and every beast that came near his grave went out of its mind and howled itself to death. The shepherd at Hvamm often came running home with Thorolf after him. One day that autumn neither sheep nor shepherd came back to the farm, and next morning, when a search was made for him, the shepherd was found dead not far from Thorolf's grave, his corpse coal-black, and every bone in his body broken. They buried him near to Thorolf. All the sheep in the valley were found dead, and the rest that had strayed into the mountains were never seen again. Any bird that happened to land on Thorolf's cairn dropped dead on the spot. All this grew so troublesome that no one would risk using the valley for grazing any longer.

At night the people at Hvamm would hear loud noises from outside, and it often sounded as if there was somebody sitting astride the roof. That winter, Thorolf often appeared on the farm, haunting his widow most of all. A lot of people suffered badly from it, but she was almost driven out of her wits, and eventually the strain of it killed her. Her body was taken up to Thorsardale to be buried beside Thorolf's cairn, and after that the people of Hvamm abandoned the farm.

Thorolf now began haunting the whole valley, and most of the farms were abandoned because of it. His ghost was so malignant that it killed people and others had to run for their lives. All those who died were later seen in his company.

Everyone complained about this reign of terror and thought it was Arnkel's business to put a stop to it. Those who thought themselves safer with Arnkel than anywhere else were invited to stay at his farm, as Thorolf and his retinue caused no harm when Arnkel was around. As the winter wore on, people grew so scared of Thorolf's ghost, they were too frightened to travel, no matter how urgent their business.

So the winter passed. Spring brought fine weather; and when all the frost in the ground had thawed, Arnkel sent a messenger over to Karsstad asking the Thorbrandssons to come and help him carry Thorolf away from Thorsardale and find him another resting-place. It was the law in those days, just as it is now, that everybody must help bury the dead if asked to give assistance. All the same, when word reached the Thorbrandssons they said they had no reason to help Arnkel and his men out of their troubles. But their father Thorbrand said, 'You ought to do whatever the law requires. You must not refuse to do what you've been asked.'

So Thorodd said to the messenger, 'Go and tell Arnkel that I'll stand in for my brothers. I'll go up to Ulfar's Fell and meet him there.'

The messenger went back and told Arnkel. He got ready at once and set out with eleven men, a few oxen, and some tools for digging. First they went up to Ulfar's Fell, where Thorodd Thorbrandsson joined them with two more men, then they all travelled together across the ridge into Thorsardale and up to Thorolf's cairn. When they broke into the cairn they saw his body was uncorrupted and very ugly to look at. They pulled him out of the grave, laid him on the sled, hitched up a powerful pair of oxen, and hauled him up as far as Ulfarsfell Ridge. By then the oxen were so exhausted they had to get another yoke of them to haul the corpse west along the ridge. Arnkel wanted to take Thorolf all the way to Vadilshofdi and bury him there, but when they came to the end of the ridge, the oxen panicked and broke loose. They ran down the ridge, then north by the hillside, past the farmstead at Ulfar's Fell, and so down to the sea, where they both collapsed. By now Thorolf had grown so heavy that the men could hardly shift him, but they managed to drag him up to a small knoll nearby, and there they buried him. This place has been known as Twist-Foot's Knoll ever since. After that Arnkel had a wall built right across the knoll just behind the grave, so high that only a bird in flight could get over it, and here Thorolf rested quietly enough as long as Arnkel lived. You can still see traces of the wall.

☙

35. NEW TROUBLES

Snorri the Priest had ignored Thorolf's protests and continued to use Krakaness Wood, but Arnkel soon made it clear that in his opinion Snorri had no legal right to it, and that by handing it over to him Thorolf had cheated his rightful heirs.

One summer Snorri sent his slaves to work in the wood. They felled a great deal of timber, stacked it up, and then went back home. When the timber had begun to dry, though Arnkel said he was going to have it collected, this was not what he did. Instead, he asked his shepherd to find out and let him know when Snorri sent for it. When the timber was dried out, Snorri sent three of his slaves for it and told his friend Hauk to go along with them for support. So they all set off, loaded the timber on twelve pack-horses, and started back home.

Arnkel's shepherd had been keeping an eye on their movements and told his master about them. Arnkel took up his weapons and set out after the slaves. He caught up with them at a place between the Svelg River and Holar. As Arnkel came up behind, Hauk jumped from his horse and thrust at him with his spear. The blow struck the shield, so he was unhurt. Arnkel jumped off his horse and drove his own spear into Hauk's belly, and ever since, the place where Hauk died has been known as the Hauk River. When the slaves saw that Hauk had been killed, they ran for home, with Arnkel chasing after them as far as the other side of Oxnabrekkur. There he turned back and drove the pack-horses up to his own farmstead. He unloaded the timber, fixed the ropes on the pack-saddles, then set the horses free, and had them driven west along the hillside to make their own way back to Helgafell. The news spread, but nothing further happened, and things stayed quiet for the rest of the year.

In the spring Snorri the Priest brought a court action over

Hauk's killing at the Thor's Ness Assembly, but Arnkel brought a counter-plea that since Hauk had been guilty of unlawful assault on him, no compensation should be paid. Each side appeared at the Assembly with a strong following, and the case was hotly contested. It was decided that since Hauk had been guilty of an unlawful assault, no compensation should be paid for him, so Snorri lost his case. After that people rode back home from the Assembly, but for the rest of the summer things remained tense.

☙

36. ATTEMPT ON ARNKEL'S LIFE

A man called Thorleif from the East Fjords had been found guilty of seduction and outlawed. He came to Helgafell in the autumn and asked Snorri the Priest to take him in. Snorri turned him away, but had a long talk with him before he left.

Thorleif went off to Bolstad, arrived there in the evening, and stayed for two nights. Next morning Arnkel was awake early repairing the main door, when Thorleif got up and asked to be taken into the household. Arnkel was not very keen and asked him if he had seen Snorri the Priest.

'I've seen him,' said Thorleif, 'and he wouldn't have me on any account. But I don't like the idea of staying with someone always likely to be on the losing side whatever he does.'

'I shouldn't have thought it much of a bargain for Snorri to give you food in return for your backing,' said Arnkel.

'I'd much rather stay here with you,' said Thorleif.

'It's not my custom to take in outsiders,' said Arnkel.

They talked the matter over for a while. Thorleif went on and on about it, while Arnkel tried to get rid of him. By this time, Arnkel had started drilling a hole through the door-plank and had laid his adze to one side. Thorleif snatched it quickly, raised it in the air and tried to drive it into Arnkel's head, but

Arnkel heard the whizz of the blow and jumped to one side, then heaved Thorleif up on his chest and soon showed him which of them was the stronger. Arnkel was a powerful man. He threw Thorleif down so hard that he was knocked almost senseless and dropped the adze. Arnkel picked it up and smashed it into Thorleif's head, striking him dead.

The rumour soon got about that Snorri the Priest had sent this man to get rid of Arnkel, but Snorri let people say whatever they liked. The rest of the year passed without further incident.

❦

37. ARNKEL IS KILLED

Next autumn, at Winter Eves,[1] Snorri the Priest gave a great feast and invited all his friends. The guests were served with ale, and there was drinking. People grew very cheerful and began comparing the farmers in the district, arguing about which of them was the best man or the greatest leader, and, as so often happens when people's abilities are being compared, there was plenty to disagree about. Most of them thought Snorri the Priest the outstanding local man, but others talked of Arnkel and some even of Styr. While they were going on about it, Thorleif Kimbi spoke up.

'What's the point of arguing?' he asked. 'We all know the truth.'

'Let's hear your opinion, then, Thorleif,' they said, 'since you're being so candid.'

1. *Vetrnætr*. The Icelandic calendar divides the year into two seasons, summer and winter. The summer always begins on a Thursday in late April, and ends on a Wednesday late in October; the winter begins on the following Saturday, and the 'Winter Eves' are those between the end of summer and the early days of winter. In pagan times sacrificial feasts used to be held about the beginning of winter.

'I think Arnkel's the greatest man of them all,' he said.

'What makes you think that?' they asked.

'Plain facts,' he said. 'As I see it, you have to take Snorri the Priest and Styr as one man because of how they're related. As for Arnkel, there hasn't been a single person in his household killed by Snorri without his getting compensation, though Snorri's mate Hauk was killed by Arnkel right by Snorri's farmstead with no payment made for him.'

Everyone thought that although Thorleif had said no more than the truth, this was going too far, considering whose house they were in, so that was the end of the argument.

As the guests were setting off from the feast, Snorri chose gifts for his friends. He went to see the Thorbrandssons off and walked them down to their ship at Raudavik Head. As they parted, Snorri had a word with Thorleif Kimbi.

'Here's an axe I'd like you to have,' he said. 'It happens to be the one with the longest handle. Should it be that you ride home to Alftafjord and take aim at Arnkel while he's stacking his hay at Orlygsstad, it might not be long enough to reach as far as his head.'

Thorleif took the axe.

'I tell you this,' he said, 'once you have made up your mind to avenge your friend Hauk, I'll not be slow to swing the axe at Arnkel's head.'

'I think you Thorbrandssons owe it to me to keep your eyes open and warn me when to go for Arnkel,' said Snorri. 'If I don't join you, when there's a chance to do something and you've given me due warning, that will be the time to start blaming me.'

And having pledged themselves to kill Arnkel, they parted. It was up to the Thorbrandssons to watch his movements.

Winter set in early with heavy frost, and all the fjords were soon frozen over. Freystein Bofi was herding sheep at Alftafjord and was supposed to look out for a chance to get at Arnkel.

Arnkel was a very hardworking man himself and made his

slaves work too, every day from sunrise to sunset. By now he was running the farms at Ulfarsfell and Orlygsstad, no one else being willing to farm there for fear of the Thorbrandssons. During the winter Arnkel used to go to Orlygsstad by moon-light for supplies of hay, but kept the slaves busy with other work during the day. It bothered him not at all that the Thorbrandssons could watch him go to haul in the hay.

One night just before Christmas Arnkel got up, roused three of his slaves, one of them called Ofeig, and went with them up to Orlygsstad along with four oxen and two sleds. The Thorbrandssons got to know about it, and that same night Freystein Bofi set off west over the ice to Helgafell. When he arrived, everyone had been in bed for some time. He roused Snorri the Priest, who asked what he wanted.

'The old eagle's flown over to his prey at Orlygsstad,' said Freystein.

Snorri got up and told his men to dress, and when they were ready they took up their weapons. Nine of them set off over the ice to Alfta Fjord. The Thorbrandssons, six-strong, joined them at the head of the fjord. They all went up to Orlygsstad, arriving just after one of the slaves had left with a hay-load. Arnkel and the two other slaves were busy getting the next load ready when they saw armed men walking up from the foreshore. Ofeig said this could only mean trouble. 'Our one chance is to get back to the farm,' he said.

'I'll tell you what,' said Arnkel. 'We'll each have to do what we think best. You two run back home and rouse my men, they'll be here in no time. The haystack's a good place to defend myself, so I'll take my stand here if these men are looking for trouble. I'd rather fight than run. They'll find me a hard man to beat, and, if you do just as I tell you, my men won't be long coming.'

As soon as Arnkel had spoken, the slaves ran off. Ofeig was the faster, and scared almost out of his wits. As he bolted up the mountain he fell over a waterfall, and that was the end of him. The place is still called Ofeig's Falls. The other slave ran all the way home. When he came to the barn, one of his fellow-slaves who was carrying in the hay called and asked him to give a hand. The slave started helping right away, and made no complaints about having to do the work.

Now we go back to Arnkel. He had recognized Snorri the Priest and others in the group, so he tore the runner off the sled and pulled it up onto the haystack. The outer turf wall was high, sloping up very steeply inwards, and the hay nearest to it had been cleared away. The place looked as safe as a fortress.

Snorri and his men came up to the haystack, it's not mentioned that many words passed between them. They set on Arnkel at once, attacking him mostly with spears, but he warded them off with the sled-runner and kept breaking their spearshafts, so he remained quite unhurt. When they ran out of missiles, Thorleif Kimbi tried scaling the wall with his drawn sword, but Arnkel struck out with the runner, and Thorleif had to jump down to avoid the blow. As the runner hit the wall, it broke the frozen turf sods and cracked at the mortise, so that one part of it fell outside the wall. Arnkel had left his sword and shield standing against the haystack, and now he took them up to defend himself. Soon he had been wounded several times but as the attackers closed in, forcing their way inside the wall, he scrambled higher up the stack. There he made his last stand, but in the end they killed him and covered his body with hay. Then Snorri took the men back to Helgafell.

Thormod Trefilsson made this verse about the killing of Arnkel:

> While yet a youth
> the battle-hard youngster
> gained victory, gorged
> and glutted the ravens:
> but Snorri's sword
> split open
> the breast of the brave
> Arnkel, his death-blow.

Coming back now to Arnkel's slaves, they finished carrying in the hay and went into the house. As they were getting out of their leather working-clothes, Arnkel's men woke up and asked where he was. The slave acted just as if he had been roused from a dream.

'The fact is,' he said, 'Arnkel must be fighting with Snorri the Priest by now, over at Orlygsstad.'

The men jumped to their feet, got into their clothes and rushed over to Orlygsstad, but found Arnkel, their master, dead. Arnkel was mourned by everyone, for of all men in pagan times he was the most gifted. He was remarkably shrewd in judgement, good-tempered, kind-hearted, brave, honest and moderate. He came out on top in every lawsuit, no matter with whom he had to deal, which explains why people were so envious of him, as is shown by the way he met his death.

Arnkel's men took his body and laid it out for burial. A mound was raised for him at Vadilshofdi close by the sea, as large as a great haystack.

☙

38. SETTLEMENT

On Arnkel's death, the legal heirs to his estate were all women, and it was their responsibility to take action over the killing. As a result the case was not followed up as vigorously as people might have expected after the killing of so great a man. The case was settled at the Assembly, and Thorleif Kimbi was the only one to be sentenced to outlawry. He was charged with giving Arnkel his death-wound and banished from Iceland for three years. Because the action over the killing of this great man had gone so badly, the leading men of Iceland made a law that neither a woman, nor a man under the age of sixteen, should ever again be allowed to raise a manslaughter action, and this has been the law ever since.

❧
39. A NEW DISPUTE

That same summer Thorleif Kimbi arranged for his passage
with some traders who were getting their ship ready in Straum
Fjord, and their leaders invited him to take meals with them. In
those days it was unusual for traders to have cooks aboard, so
all those who messed together would cast lots from day to day
to decide which of them should do the cooking. There was a
common supply of water for the whole crew from a cask with a
lid on it, which stood near the mast. Extra water was kept in
barrels and emptied into the cask as the water there was used
up.

As they were just about to set sail, a stranger came down to
Budarhamar, a tall man carrying a bundle on his back, with
something out of the ordinary about him. He asked for the
skipper and was shown to his tent. The stranger laid his
bundle down by the tent door, went inside, and asked the
skipper if he would take him abroad. When they asked him his
name, he said he was Arnbjorn Asbrandsson of Kamb and
wanted to go abroad to look for his brother Bjorn, who had left
the country some years before, and about whom nothing had
been heard since he went to Denmark. The traders said they
had already covered up the cargo and didn't want to re-open it.
Arnbjorn pointed out that he had so little baggage it could
easily be placed on top of the cargo. It seemed to them he had
urgent reasons for going overseas, so they took him aboard. As
he was alone and not sharing meals with anybody, he was
given a berth in the bows. His baggage consisted of three
hundred ells of homespun cloth, twelve sheepskins, and food
for the voyage. Arnbjorn proved very handy and helpful, and
the traders came to like him a lot.

They had a good passage, and after making landfall in
Hordaland, they sailed up to a rocky island and went ashore to

cook a meal. It was Thorleif's turn to do the cooking, and he was supposed to make porridge. Arnbjorn was already ashore, cooking porridge for himself in the pot that Thorleif was to use after him. Thorleif went ashore and told Arnbjorn to give him the pot, but the porridge was not quite ready, and Arnbjorn stirred away, refusing to budge. The Norwegians on board started shouting at Thorleif, telling him to get on with the cooking. They said he was just like all the other Icelanders, far too slow at everything. Thorleif got into a temper, grabbed the pot and flung it down, spilling Arnbjorn's porridge, but as Thorleif started walking away, Arnbjorn hit him on the neck with the ladle which he still had in his hand. It was not a hard blow, but the ladle was hot with the porridge and burnt Thorleif's neck.

'Since we're the only Icelanders here,' said Thorleif, 'it wouldn't be right to give the Norwegians a chance to make fun of us, and drag us apart like a pair of fighting dogs. But I'll remember this next time we meet back in Iceland.' Arnbjorn made no reply.

They lay there at anchor for some days till they got a favourable wind to take them up to the mainland, and there they unloaded the cargo. Thorleif found lodgings, but Arnbjorn fixed himself up with a passage on a cargo boat bound for Oslo Fjord. From there he sailed to Denmark and started looking for his brother Bjorn.

❧

40. BJORN COMES BACK TO ICELAND

Thorleif Kimbi spent two years in Norway, then went back to Iceland with the same traders. They made landfall at Breida Fjord and sailed up to Dogurdar Ness. Thorleif came home to Alftafjord that autumn, as pleased with himself as ever.

That same summer Bjorn and his brother Arnbjorn also came back to Iceland, and landed at Hraunhaven Mouth. By this time Bjorn had the nickname of Breidavik-Champion. Arnbjorn came back with a good deal of money, and shortly afterwards bought some land at Bakki in Hraun Haven. He started farming there the following spring after having spent the winter with his brother-in-law, Thord Blig. Arnbjorn was not a man for display, and had little to say for himself, but at the same time he was a man of great courage. His brother Bjorn, on the other hand, was the one for show, and after he came back to Iceland he used to dress well, after the fashion of people of distinction overseas. He was also much more handsome than Arnbjorn, but no less courageous, and he had picked up a lot of battle experience while he was abroad.

That summer, shortly after their return, people crowded to a gathering at Haugabrekkur east of the mouth of Frod River on the north side of the moor. The traders came to it on horseback, all dressed in brightly coloured clothes, and by the time they arrived a lot of people had already gathered. Among them was Thurid, the housewife at Frodriver, and Bjorn went over to have a word with her. No one thought anything of it. It seemed only natural that they should have plenty to talk about when they had seen nothing of each other for such a long time.

Later in the day a fight broke out at the meeting, and one of the men from the north side received a fatal wound. People carried him into a willow copse on the flats by the river. The wound was bleeding freely, and a pool of blood formed beside the thicket. Young Kjartan, Thurid's son, had a small axe in his hand. He ran up to the willows and dipped the axe in the blood.

After the meeting, when the people from the south were riding back home, Thord Blig asked Bjorn how he had got on with Thurid, and Bjorn said he was quite pleased with the talk they'd had. Thord asked if he had noticed young Kjartan, the son of Thurid and Thorodd – and someone else?

'I saw him,' said Bjorn.

'What do you think of him, then?' asked Thord, and Bjorn replied with this verse:

> I saw the boy,
> his eyes ablaze,
> walk like a wolf
> to the blood-pool by the willows.
> He's my living likeness
> but little does he know
> that the ship's steersman
> is his seafaring sire.

'Thorodd must be wondering whether he's the boy's father or you are,' said Thord, and Bjorn made another verse:

> The slim, well-bred woman
> who bears Thorodd's weight
> sought me once, sweetly
> with her soft body.
> Brooding, I yearn
> that her body might breed
> more boys like the brave lad
> born in my image.

'Best not have anything more to do with Thurid,' said Thord, 'try to forget her.'

'That makes sense,' said Bjorn, 'but my heart tells me otherwise, though I know I'll be up against someone I'm no match for, and that's her brother, Snorri the Priest.'

'Look out for yourself,' said Thord, and that was the end of their conversation.

Bjorn went to live at Kamb and took charge of the farm, as his father was dead by this time. That winter he set off north across the moor to see Thurid. Thorodd took it very badly, but didn't see what he could do about it. He kept thinking of the difficult time the two of them had given him before, when he complained about how they were carrying on. Now he realized that Bjorn was a more formidable rival than ever. That winter Thorodd gave Thorgrima Witch-Face some money to work a spell and cause a blizzard when Bjorn was crossing the moor.

One day Bjorn went over to Frodriver. In the evening when he started back, the sky was overcast, and it rained a little. He was late leaving, and by the time he got up to the moor the weather had grown colder, and snow was drifting. It soon grew too dark for him to see the path, and then a blizzard blew up, so violent that he could hardly stay on his feet. He was soaked to the skin, and now his clothes began to freeze, he had lost his bearings and had no idea where he was going. During the night he came upon a cave and crawled inside to shelter there till morning, but it was cold comfort. Then he made this verse:

> The woman, so warm,
> asleep in her wide bed
> would shiver with pity
> could she picture my plight;
> her loving seafarer
> must lie alone,
> cold, without comfort,
> in his rocky cave.

He added another:

> Since she swore me
> her love I've sailed
> my laden ship
> through sharp seas:
> many the burden
> that I've borne bravely.
> Now I must barter
> her bed for this burrow.

Bjorn spent three days in the cave before the weather cleared up. On the fourth day he made his way down from the moor and back home to Kamb in a state of complete exhaustion. People asked him where he had been during the blizzard, and he made this verse:

> You've heard of my bold spirit
> 'neath Styrbjorn's standard
> when the iron-clad Eirik
> ambled through blood?
> But now I've wandered
> away into the wilderness,
> lost my bearings
> in that black blizzard.

Bjorn stayed at home for the rest of the winter. In the spring his brother Arnbjorn started farming at Bakki in Hraun Haven, but Bjorn went on living at Kamb and ran a splendid farm.

❦

41. A MARRIAGE OFFER

That spring at the Thor's Ness Assembly, Thorleif Kimbi made an offer of marriage and asked for the hand of Helga, Thorlak's-daughter, sister of Steinthor of Eyr. Her brother Thormod was strongly in favour, as he was married to Thorleif Kimbi's sister Thorgerd, but when Steinthor was told, he seemed not very keen and asked his brothers what they thought about it. First they went to Thord Blig, and when the matter was put to him, this is what he said:

'I'm not waiting to hear what other people want, and I shan't mince my words. I'll tell you this to your face, Thorleif, I'll never see my sister married to you until the scars are healed that you got on your neck from that porridge in Norway three years ago.'

'I'm not sure what can be done about that,' said Thorleif, 'and I doubt if I'll be able to take my revenge. But I'll say this: before the next three years are out, I'd very much like to see you get a knock yourself.'

'You don't scare me with your threats,' said Thord.

Next morning there was a turf-game[1] going on near the Thorbrandssons' tent. The Thorlakssons happened to be passing by, when a great lump of sandy turf came flying through the air and caught Thord Blig on the neck, hitting him so hard that he went head over heels. When he got back on his feet again, he could see the Thorbrandssons laughing at him. The Thorlakssons turned with their swords drawn, and the two sides faced up to each other and began fighting. Several were wounded, but no one was killed. Steinthor was not involved, as he was off somewhere else talking with Snorri the Priest. The fighters were separated, and people tried to arrange a settlement. In the end it was agreed that Snorri and Steinthor should arbitrate, and their verdict was that the wounds on either side and the unlawful assault should cancel each other out, with compensation to be paid where things needed to be evened up. So when they rode back home, they had more or less come to terms.

❦

42. ATTEMPT ON ARNBJORN'S LIFE

That summer a ship put in at Hraunhaven Mouth, and another at Dogurdar Ness. Snorri the Priest had some business with the ship at Hraun Haven, so he rode off with fourteen companions. As they were coming south over the moor on their way into Dufgusdale, six fully armed men came after them, riding hard. It was the Thorbrandssons. When Snorri asked where they were heading, they said they were on their way to the ship at Hraunhaven Mouth. Snorri offered to look after their business there. He asked them to go back home and take care not to provoke anyone, as very little was needed to spark

---

1. This game is not mentioned anywhere else, and how it was played is not known.

off trouble between people on uneasy terms should they happen to meet.

'No one's going to say we're too frightened of the men of Breidavik to travel through the district,' said Thorleif Kimbi. 'Of course, you can ride back home yourself, if you're too timid to go about your own business.'

Snorri made no answer, and together they rode on across the ridges west to Hofgardar, and from there by the shore route over the sands. As they were coming towards the estuary, the Thorbrandssons turned off up towards Bakki and dismounted at the farmstead. They tried to force their way into the house, but couldn't break open the door, so they climbed onto the roof and started tearing it off. Inside the house, Arnbjorn had his weapons ready to defend himself. He kept thrusting his spear through the roof, and his attackers suffered several wounds. It was early morning, and the day was fine and sunny.

That same morning the men of Breidavik had got up early and set off towards the ship. As they were passing Oxl, they noticed someone in bright clothes on top of the farmhouse roof at Bakki. They knew it was not Arnbjorn's style of dress, so Bjorn and his men rode up to the farmstead.

As soon as Snorri the Priest realized the Thorbrandssons were not with him any longer, he rode back after them; and when he and his men came to Bakki, the Thorbrandssons were still busy trying to break through the roof. Snorri told the brothers to clear off and not cause any trouble as long as they were with him. Since they had not managed to get into the house, they did as they were told, gave up the attack, and rode with him down to the ship.

The men of Breidavik got to the ship later in the day. The two sides kept out of each other's way, and though there was a lot of strain and tension between them, they didn't come to blows. The men of Breidavik outnumbered their opponents at the market. In the evening Snorri the Priest rode south to Hofgardar, where Bjorn and his son Gest were living at the time – Gest was the father of Hofgardar-Ref. Bjorn the Breidavik-Champion and his men told Arnbjorn they were ready to ride after Snorri, but Arnbjorn was against it and said it would be best if both sides were to rest content with the points they had scored already. Snorri and his party rode back home the following day, the Thorbrandssons even more unhappy about things than before. So the autumn passed.

❧

43. THE PRICE OF A SLAVE

Thorbrand of Alftafjord had a slave called Egil the Strong, exceptionally big and powerful. He did not enjoy being a slave, so he kept begging Thorbrand and his sons to give him his freedom, and promised to do anything within his power to repay them. One evening Egil went to herd his sheep between Alfta Fjord and Borgardale. It was getting very late, when he saw an eagle come flying east across the fjord. Egil had a big foxhound with him. The eagle came swooping down, picked up the dog in its talons, and flew with it west across the fjord to Thorolf's grave. Then the eagle flew on and vanished behind the mountain. Thorbrand said it was an omen that something was about to happen.

At Winter Eves it was the custom of the Breidavik people to hold ball games just below Oxl Mountain, south of Knorr, and the place is still known as the Leikskalar Fields.[1] People from all over the district would come to these games in crowds, and large shelters were built for them there, as some of them would stay for a fortnight or even longer. At that time there were a

---

1. *Leik-skálar*, literally 'playing-sheds'. These ball games were played in winter, on ice. A wooden ball was used, and the object of the game seems to have been to get the ball across the opponents' line: but the rules are not known in detail.

good many people living in the district, among them some
very fine men. Most of the younger men took part in the
games, but not Thord Blig. It was not so much his strength as
his aggressiveness that made them keep him out of the games,
so he used to sit on a stool and watch the play. Bjorn and his
brother Arnbjorn were so strong, people thought they ought
not to play unless they competed against each other.

That same autumn the Thorbrandssons told their slave Egil
to go to the ball-games and find a way to kill one of the
Breidavik men, either Bjorn, Arnbjorn, or Thord. In return
they promised him his freedom. Some people think that Snorri
the Priest was behind the plot, and that it was his idea that the
slave should hide in the shed and attack his victim there.
Snorri is said to have told the slave to wait in the mountain pass
above Leikskalar and not go down from there till the fires had
been lit, as there is usually a sea-breeze in the evening which
would carry the smoke up to the mountain pass. People say he
warned Egil to wait there and not go down till the mountain
pass had filled with smoke.

Egil set out on his mission. First he travelled west to the
fjords, where he kept asking about the Alftafjord sheep and
pretended to be searching for them, though Freystein Bofi was
herding them all the time at Alftafjord.

In the evening, after Egil had gone, Freystein went across
the river to keep an eye on the sheep and when he came west of
the river to the scree called Geirvör[2] which stretches across it,
he saw a severed human head. The head was chanting this
verse:

> Red with gore
> are Geirvör's lips:
> soon she'll kiss
> the skulls of
> men.

2. Geirvör is not only the name of the scree but also a woman's name. The
second element, *vör*, can mean a lip.

He told Thorbrand about this, and Thorbrand thought it very ominous.

Meanwhile Egil kept on the move, west through the fjords, up the mountain east of Buland Head, then south straight across the mountain into the pass above Leikskalar, and there he hid for the rest of the day, watching the games being played.

Thord Blig was not taking part, but was sitting at the games. 'I'm not sure what it is I keep seeing up there in the pass,' he said. 'It's either a bird or someone in hiding. It keeps bobbing up and down. It must be alive. I think it would be a good idea to take a closer look.' But nobody did anything about it.

That day it was the turn of Bjorn the Breidavik-Champion and Thord Blig to do the chores at the shed. Bjorn's job was to light the fire and Thord's to fetch the water. When Bjorn had the fire going, the smoke started drifting up to the mountain pass, just as Snorri had said it would, and Egil set off down to the shed under cover of the smoke. The games were still on, though it was getting very late. The fire was blazing away, and when the shed was full of smoke, Egil made his way down to it, very stiff from his wait on the mountain. He was wearing shoes with tasselled thongs, as people did in those days, and one of the thongs came undone, so the tassel was trailing behind him as he walked into the big shed. He tried to tread as softly as he could, for he had already caught a glimpse of Thord and Bjorn sitting by the fire, and thought he had a lifetime of freedom within his grasp, but as he crossed the doorsill, he stepped on the loose tassel. He tried to move the other foot, but the tassel was caught, so that he tripped and crashed onto the floor with a great thump that sounded like the carcass of a skinned bull being thrown down. Thord leapt to his feet and asked who the devil was there. Bjorn was up, too, and pounced on Egil. Before he could get to his feet, Bjorn had taken hold of him and was asking him his name.

'It's Egil, friend,' said the slave.

'Egil who?' asked Bjorn.

'Egil of Alftafjord,' he said.

Thord picked up a sword, and would have killed him, had Bjorn not held him back and told him to do nothing yet. 'First we must get the whole story out of him,' he said.

They shackled Egil by the feet; and when people came back to the shed in the evening, Egil told all of them what he had been sent to do. They kept him there overnight, and in the morning took him up to the pass and killed him. Nowadays the place is called Egilsskard.[3]

It was the law in those days that anyone who killed another man's slave was to bring the owner twelve ounces of silver to his home in compensation. He should set out not later than sunrise on the third day after the killing. Once this payment had been properly made, no legal action could be taken.

After they had put Egil to death, the Breidavik brothers decided to hand over compensation as the law demanded. They set out from Leikskalar with thirty hand-picked men and rode north over the moor to see Steinthor of Eyr, where they stayed overnight. He came along with them, and by the time they set off from Eyr they were sixty strong. They rode east by the fjords and spent the next night at Bakki with Steinthor's brother Thormod. They asked their kinsmen Styr and Vermund to join them, so by now there were eighty of them altogether. Steinthor sent someone over to Helgafell to see what Snorri would do when he found out about the force they had gathered. When the spy came to Helgafell, Snorri was sitting in the high-seat, and there was nothing out of the ordinary to show what Snorri was planning to do. He returned to Bakki and told Steinthor what he had seen at Helgafell.

'It's just as I thought,' said Steinthor. 'Snorri would never deny us our legal rights, and if he's not going to Alftafjord, I don't see any point in taking this large force with us, for I want us to go about our business quietly and complete it legally. I think it would be a good idea if you, Thord, and the rest of the

3. Literally, 'Egil's pass'.

Breidavik men were to stay behind, because the smallest thing could spark off a fight between you and the Thorbrandssons.'

'I'm going and that's a fact,' said Thord. 'Thorleif Kimbi's not going to have an excuse to poke fun at me and say I'd never dare to bring the slave-payment myself.'

Steinthor turned to the brothers Bjorn and Arnbjorn and said, 'I want you to stay behind with twenty men.'

'I'm not going to force you to take me along if you don't want me,' said Bjorn, 'but this is the first war-band I've ever been thrown out of. One thing I do know. Snorri the Priest will outsmart you all, for though I'm no prophet, I've an inkling of how your trip's going to turn out. Next time we meet, you'll be telling me you didn't have enough men with you.'

'As long as I'm in charge here, I'll follow my own counsel,' said Steinthor, 'even though I may not be as smart as Snorri the Priest.'

'You can do whatever you like, kinsman, for all I care,' said Bjorn.

After that Steinthor set off from Bakki with nearly sixty men. They rode east across Skeid over to Drapuhlid, then on to Vatnshals, right across Svelgsradale and up to Ulfarsfell Ridge.

44. THE BATTLE OF ALFTA FJORD

Snorri the Priest had sent word asking his neighbours to move their ships to leeward of Raudavik Head, and as soon as Steinthor's spy was out of the way, he set off to join them with his men. He chose not to go sooner, as he knew Steinthor must have sent this man to spy on him. Snorri sailed three ships up Alfta Fjord with nearly fifty men aboard, and reached Karsstad ahead of Steinthor. When they saw Steinthor's force moving towards Karsstad, the Thorbrandssons wanted to march against them and block their way into the home meadow. 'We've plenty of good fighting men here,' they said. There were eighty of them all told.

'We must neither bar them from the farmstead nor refuse Steinthor his legal rights,' said Snorri the Priest. 'I know he'll go about his business in a quiet and sensible manner, so let's all go inside. I don't want anybody to start bandying words with them, since that would only make matters worse.'

They went into the living-room, and all sat down on the benches except the Thorbrandssons, who kept pacing up and down the floor. Steinthor and his men came riding up to the door. People say he wore a scarlet tunic tucked into his belt at the front. He had a fine shield and helmet, and at his waist a splendidly ornamented sword: the hilt shone with white silver, and the grip was bound with silver wire, gold-threaded. After Steinthor and his men had dismounted, he walked up to the door, and nailed to it a purse containing twelve ounces of silver. Then he appointed witnesses to testify that he had made lawful payment for the slave.

The door was open, and one of the women was standing there listening to the naming of witnesses. She went into the room. 'That Steinthor's a fine-looking warrior,' she said. 'When he paid the compensation for the slave, he spoke really well.'

As soon as Thorleif Kimbi heard this, he rushed out of the room with his brothers. The rest of the men followed but Thorleif was the first to get to the door. He saw Thord Blig standing outside holding a shield in front of him, while Steinthor had already started off across the home meadow. Thorleif grabbed a spear standing by the door and lunged at Thord. It struck the shield, but glanced off into the shoulder, giving him a nasty wound. Now the rest of the men came running out, and a battle started in the meadow near the farmstead. Steinthor was making a real fight of it, hewing away on either side. Then Snorri the Priest came out and told them to stop. He asked Steinthor to ride away from the meadow and promised not to go after him, so Steinthor and his men left the field and the fighting ended.

As Snorri came back to the door, he saw his son Thorodd standing there with a bad shoulder wound. He was just twelve years old. Snorri asked who had given him the wound.

'Steinthor of Eyr,' said the boy.

'Steinthor seems to have done his best to pay you back for your promise not to go after him,' said Thorleif Kimbi. 'I don't think we should let him get away with this.'

'Very well,' said Snorri. 'We've not done with him yet.'

He asked Thorleif to tell the others that they were going after Steinthor and his men, who had just left the home meadow when they saw people coming after them. They crossed the river and made their way up the scree called Geirvör. It was an ideal place to make a stand because of the stones lying everywhere, and there they braced themselves for the fight. As Snorri and his men were coming up the scree, Steinthor cast a spear over them for good luck, according to ancient custom.[1] The spear sought out its victim and struck Mar Hallvardsson, Snorri's uncle, putting him out of the fight. They told Snorri about this. 'Good,' he said, 'that shows it's not always best to walk behind.'

Then the fighting started in real earnest. Steinthor was always in front, hewing away on either side, but whenever he struck a shield, his ornamented sword would bend, and he had to put his foot on it to straighten it out. He did his best to get at Snorri the Priest. His kinsman Styr Thorgrimsson fought spiritedly at his side, and it was he who claimed the first victim when he killed a man on Snorri's, his own son-in-law's, side. Snorri saw it happen. 'Is this how you avenge your grandson Thorodd,' he asked, 'when he's dying of the wound Steinthor gave him? You're no better than a traitor!'

1. The ancient custom of casting a spear over the enemy ranks is associated elsewhere in medieval Icelandic literature with the cult of Odin, the god of war, to whom the victims were dedicated: see, *e.g.*, *Styrbjorn's Saga* and *The Sybil's Vision*.

'I can soon make it up to you,' said Styr, and with that he changed sides. He joined Snorri with all his followers, and the next man he killed was one of Steinthor's.

Then Aslak of Langadale came on the scene with his son Illugi the Strong and thirty men, and tried to stop the fighting. Vermund the Slender joined with them, and they all appealed to Snorri to put an end to this slaughter. Snorri replied that it was up to the men of Eyr to come forward and make peace with him, and the mediators asked Steinthor to accept a truce on behalf of his men. Steinthor asked Snorri to shake hands on the agreement, but just as Snorri stretched out his hand, Steinthor drew his sword and struck at it. The sword landed with a loud crack on the temple-ring and cut it almost in two, but Snorri was unhurt.

'They'll never keep the peace,' shouted Thorodd Thorbrandsson, 'we'll have to go on fighting till all the Thorlakssons are dead.'

'There'll be plenty of trouble in this neighbourhood, if all the Thorlakssons have to die,' said Snorri the Priest. 'So if Steinthor's willing, we'd better come to terms as we've already agreed.'

Everyone pleaded with Steinthor to make peace, and in the end a truce was arranged for each man to go safely back home.

When the men of Breidavik heard that Snorri had taken a large force of men with him to Alftafjord, they set out on horseback after Steinthor, riding as hard as they could, and while the battle on the scree was being fought, they were making their way along the ridge above Ulfarsfell. Some people say Snorri the Priest had already caught sight of Bjorn and his men on the ridge as he was facing that way, which is why he was so ready to make peace with Steinthor.

After the battle Steinthor and Bjorn met at Orlygsstad, and Bjorn said it had turned out just as he had predicted. 'Now I think we should turn back and hit them hard,' he said.

'Whatever might happen between us in the future,' said Steinthor, 'I shall hold to my agreement with Snorri the Priest.'

Then they rode off each to his own home, apart from Thord Blig who had to stay in bed at Eyr while his wounds were healing.

Five of Steinthor's men were killed in the Battle of Alfta Fjord and Snorri the Priest lost two, but many on both sides were wounded, for the fighting had been bitter. This is how Thormod Trefilsson described it in his *Lay of the Raven*:

> The feaster of ravens
> fed to the eagles flesh,
> fit that food
> for wolves at Alfta Fjord!
> Five of those fighters
> fell to Snorri,
> in the flashing of the war-storm
> were his foes defeated.

Along with Aslak and Illugi, Thorbrand had been at the battle in the role of peacemaker, and it was he who asked them to seek a settlement. He thanked the other two generously for the help they had given, and Snorri for his support. After the battle Snorri the Priest went back to Helgafell. The agreement was that, until the quarrel had been settled, the Thorbrandssons should stay alternately at Helgafell or home at Alftafjord, because feeling still ran high between the two sides, and the truce was not binding once the men were back home after the battle.

45. THE BATTLE OF VIGRA FJORD

As we have said already, the summer before the Battle of Alfta Fjord a ship put in at Dogurdar Ness. Steinthor of Eyr had bought a fine ten-oared boat there, and as he was sailing to fetch it, he ran into a fierce westerly gale which drove him round Thor's Ness and forced him to put in at Thingskalar

Ness. They hauled the boat ashore at Gruflu-Naust, and from there they travelled on foot across the hills over to Bakki and the rest of the way by sea. They did not get round to fetching the ten-oared boat that autumn, and it lay at Gruflu-Naust, where they had left it.

Early one morning just before Christmas, Steinthor got up and said he was going over to Thingskalar Ness for the boat. His brothers Bergthor and Thord Blig went with him. Thord's wounds had healed so well that he could fight again. Two Norwegians were staying with Steinthor, and they joined him on the trip so there were eight of them altogether. First they had themselves ferried across the fjord over to Selja Head, and from there they walked on to Bakki, where their brother Thormod joined them, so they were now nine strong.

Hofstad Bay was frozen over as far out as Greater Bakki, so they walked across the ice, and then over the isthmus to Vigra Fjord, which was also under ice. This fjord dries up at low tide, and then the ice settles on the mud flats, but the rocks in the fjord stick up through the ice. Slabs of broken ice were jutting up all round the rocks, and the ice was covered with a layer of fresh snow, making it very slippery.

Steinthor and his men walked over to Thingskalar and hauled the boat down from the shed. They took the oars and benches from the boat, left them on the ice with their heavy weapons and clothes, and began dragging the boat north across the fjord over the isthmus to Hofstad Bay right to the edge of the ice. Then they turned back to get their clothes and other things they had left behind. Just as they reached Vigra Fjord, they saw six men travelling fast across the ice from Thingskalar Ness towards Helgafell, and suspected they would be the Thorbrandssons. Steinthor's party began running across the fjord to get their clothes and weapons. As Steinthor had guessed, they were the Thorbrandssons alright. When the Thorbrandssons saw people running across the fjord, they too realized who these men must be. They knew

Steinthor and his men would be keen to face them, and they decided to make their stand. The two parties came very close to each other, but the Thorbrandssons were the first to get to the rock. As soon as Steinthor and his men came close enough, Thorleif Kimbi threw a spear which hit Bergthor Thorlaksson in the belly and put him out of the fight. Bergthor walked a few steps over the ice and lay down, but Steinthor and some of his men made an attack on the rock, while others ran back to arm themselves. The Thorbrandssons put up stout resistance. They were in a strong position with the slippery ice blocks on all sides of the rock, so none of them was wounded until the others came back with the weapons. Steinthor and another five men tried a direct assault, but the Norwegians held back and shot at those on the rock with their bows and arrows. They soon began to wound the defenders.

Thorleif saw Steinthor drawing his sword. 'I see you're still wearing a white-hilted sword, Steinthor,' he said, 'I wonder, has it the same blunt edge as the one you carried last autumn at Alftafjord?'

'I'd like to try out the sword on you before we part,' said Steinthor, 'and then we'll see how blunt it is.'

They found the rock difficult to attack. After they had been fighting for some time, Thord Blig ran up to it and tried to lunge with a spear at Thorleif Kimbi, who was always to the fore. Thorleif took the spear on his shield, but the thrust was so powerful that Thord slipped on the sloping ice block, fell backwards, and slid away down from the rock. Thorleif rushed after him, meaning to kill him before he could get back on his feet. Wearing spiked shoes Freystein Bofi ran forward to join Thorleif, and Steinthor moved quickly towards them. He flung his shield over Thord as Thorleif was about to strike, and with his other hand he took a swing at Thorleif, severing the leg just below the knee. At that same moment Freystein Bofi made a thrust at Steinthor's belly, but Steinthor saw it coming and leapt in the air so that the spear went between his legs. All three things Steinthor did simultaneously, just as we've described. Then he struck at Freystein with his sword, and the blow landed on his neck with a loud crack.

'A nasty one, that, Freystein,' said Steinthor.

'Yes, it was,' agreed Freystein, 'but not as bad as you thought, it's done me no harm.' He was wearing a felt hood with a piece of horn sewn onto the collar, where the blow had landed.

Freystein started back to the rock, but Steinthor told him not to run if he wasn't hurt, so Freystein turned and they attacked each other again. Steinthor kept skidding off balance because the blocks of ice were steep and slippery, while Freystein stood firm on his spikes and was able to strike hard at him again and again, but at last Steinthor got in a blow just above Freystein's hips, slicing him clear through. Then they all moved up to the rock and there was no stopping them till all the Thorbrandssons were down. Thord Blig wanted them to cut off the Thorbrandssons' heads, but Steinthor said he would not make war on men who were on their backs. So now they moved away from the rock over to where Bergthor lay. He could still talk, and they took him back with them over the ice, across the isthmus and to the boat, then rowed over to Bakki in the evening.

That day Snorri's shepherd had been at Oxnabrekkur and could see the fighting on Vigra Fjord. He raced back home and told Snorri that a terrible battle was taking place there. Snorri and his men, nine of them altogether, took up their weapons and went over to the fjord. By the time they got there, Steinthor and his men were already away from the ice-field. When Snorri went to look at the wounded, he saw that while only Freystein Bofi was dead, all the others were so badly hurt they seemed unlikely to live. Thorleif Kimbi called out to Snorri, urging him to go after Steinthor and not let any of them get away alive. Snorri went over to the spot where Bergthor had been lying and saw a large clot of blood. He picked up a lump of snow mixed with blood, squeezed it, and put it up to his mouth. Then he asked whose blood it was, and Thorleif

Kimbi said it was Bergthor's. Snorri said this was blood from an internal wound.

'You're probably right,' said Thorleif. 'He was hit by a spear.'

'As I see it,' said Snorri, 'it's a dying man's blood, so we needn't go after them.'

They carried the Thorbrandssons over to Helgafell, where their wounds were seen to. Thorodd Thorbrandsson had a deep cut on his neck and was unable to hold his head straight. He was wearing tight-fitting breeches, and they were soaked with blood. One of Snorri's men tried to help him undress, but no matter how hard he tugged, there was no way he could pull off the breeches.

'They're not exaggerating when they talk about your taste in clothes,' said the man. 'You Thorbrandssons wear such a tight fit they won't come off.'

'Then you can't be pulling hard enough,' said Thorodd.

The man braced his feet against the bench and gave another tug at the breeches as hard as he could, but still they would not come off. Then Snorri the Priest came up and felt the leg, and saw that a spear was stuck right through it between the tendon and the shin-bone, skewering the trousers to the leg. Snorri said the man was remarkably stupid not to have noticed.

Snorri Thorbrandsson was the fittest of the brothers, and in the evening he sat down at table with Snorri the Priest. There was cheese and curds for supper. Snorri the Priest thought his namesake was not doing justice to the cheese, and asked why he was eating so slowly. Snorri Thorbrandsson said lambs gagged for weaning were usually poor eaters. Snorri the Priest felt his throat and found an arrow sticking right through at the base of the tongue. He got a pair of pincers and pulled it out, after which Snorri Thorbrandsson could take his food again.

Snorri the Priest was able to heal all the Thorbrandssons' wounds. When Thorodd's neck began to heal, his head was a little to one side and he said Snorri was turning him into a cripple, but Snorri said he was sure the neck would straighten up once the sinews began to knit. Thorodd wanted to have the wound re-opened and the head set straighter, but it turned out just as Snorri had said, and once the sinews knit, Thorodd's head straightened up. All the same, Thorodd still found it hard to bend his head even a little.

Thorleif Kimbi walked with a wooden leg for the rest of his life.

☙

46. SETTLEMENT

Steinthor of Eyr and his men rowed to the boat-shed at Bakki and hauled the boat ashore. Two of the brothers were able to walk up to the farmstead, but they had to leave Bergthor behind and kept him there overnight in a tent. The story goes that Thormod's wife, Thorgerd, would not go to bed with her husband that evening, but then someone came up from the boat-shed and told them Bergthor was dead. When Thorgerd heard this she went to bed as usual, and from what people say, there is no report of any further disagreement between her and her husband. Steinthor went back home to Eyr in the morning, and for the rest of the winter things stayed quiet in the district.

In the spring, as Summons Days were drawing nearer, people of goodwill thought it a terrible thing for such great and close neighbours to remain enemies and keep fighting one another; and so good men, friendly to both sides, tried to bring about a settlement between them. Vermund the Slender acted as spokesman, and had the backing of a number of good-natured people related to both parties. Eventually a truce was arranged between them, and then they were reconciled. Most people agree it was Vermund who acted as arbitrator and announced the verdict at the Thor's Ness Assembly with all the wisest men at his side. According to the terms of the settlement, the killings and assaults on both sides were paired

off. It was agreed that the wound Thord Blig received at Alfta
Fjord should cancel the one given to Thorodd Snorrason. Mar
Hallvardsson's wound and the blow Steinthor gave Snorri the
Priest were said to equal the deaths of the three men killed at
Alfta Fjord. The killings by Styr, one on either side, cancelled
each other out, as did the killing of Bergthor and the wounds of
the Thorbrandssons in the fight on Vigra Fjord. The killing of
Freystein Bofi was set against the killing of one of Steinthor's
men at Alfta Fjord. Thorleif Kimbi got compensation for the leg
he had lost. The killing of one of Snorri's men at Alfta Fjord
was matched against the unlawful assault Thorleif Kimbi had
committed by starting the fight. All other injuries were evened
out, all outstanding differences paid for, and so they parted on
friendly terms. Everyone honoured this settlement as long as
Steinthor and Snorri were both alive.

☙

47. ATTEMPT ON BJORN'S LIFE

That same summer, after the settlement, Thorodd the Tribute-
Trader invited his brother-in-law Snorri the Priest to a feast at
Frodriver, and Snorri came with eight companions. During the
feast Thorodd complained to him about the shame and humiliation he had suffered from Bjorn Asbrandsson's visits to his
wife Thurid, Snorri's sister. Thorodd said he thought it
Snorri's duty to put a stop to this embarrassing business.
Snorri was at the feast for several days, and Thorodd gave him
some fine gifts when they parted. From there Snorri rode
south across the moor, saying he was on his way to the ship at
Hraunhaven Mouth. This was during the haymaking season.

When they came south to Kamb Moor, Snorri said, 'Now
we're going to ride down from the moor to Kamb, and I want
you to know what I've decided. We're going to attack Bjorn
and kill him if we can, but there aren't enough of us to get him

in his own house – it's too well built and he's a brave, strong man. Even with a force much stronger than ours, people have always found it hard to overcome a man as strong as he is, if he's inside a house. Take the case of Gizur the Priest and Gizur the White, when eighty of them attacked Gunnar of Hlidarend at his home. Though he was fighting alone, he killed some and wounded others, and they'd have given up the attack if Geir the Priest hadn't been clever enough to see that Gunnar was running out of arrows.[1] Now if Bjorn should be out of doors, as you'd expect in such fine drying weather, I want you to take him, Mar, but look out for yourself, Bjorn isn't a man to be trifled with, and unless we deal him his death-blow very fast, you can expect a hard fight from that killer-wolf.'

They made their way down from the moor and rode straight to the farmstead, where they saw Bjorn in the home meadow making a hay-sled. He was on his own, with no weapons except a small adze and a big knife he was using to widen the mortises in the runners, its blade a span long.

Bjorn watched the riders coming down from the moor into the meadow, and recognized them at once with Snorri the Priest in the lead wearing a blue cloak. Then Bjorn made a daring move. He picked up the knife and walked straight towards them. When he got to Snorri, he took hold of his cloak-sleeve with one hand and pointed the knife right at Snorri's chest with the other, ready to drive it home directly. He greeted them, and Snorri returned his greeting, but Mar lost his nerve when he saw how easily Bjorn could stab Snorri if anyone tried to rush him. Bjorn walked them on their way and asked the news, without relaxing the firm grip he had on Snorri.

'So it's come to this, Snorri,' said Bjorn. 'I can't deny it, I've done things to offend you, and you have good reason to hold them against me. I've heard of the grudge you bear me, and I

---

1. An allusion to Gunnar's heroic last fight, described in *Njal's Saga*, pp. 169–71.

want you to tell me now whether you're here for a purpose or just passing by. If you want to see me, you'd better tell me why, otherwise give your word to leave me in peace, and I'll go back home. Nobody's going to make a fool of me.'

'This meeting of ours has turned out so well for you,' said Snorri, 'that I'll have to spare your life, no matter what I had in mind before we met. But I want to ask you to stop playing around with my sister Thurid. We'll never be on good terms while you carry on like this.'

'I'll not promise you anything I can't carry out,' said Bjorn, 'and I'm not sure it's a promise I can honour while I'm living in the same neighbourhood as Thurid.'

'There's not much to keep you here,' said Snorri, 'you can easily leave the district.'

'You're right,' said Bjorn, 'and since you've come to see me about it, I'll do as you suggest. Our meeting is over now, but I promise you, neither Thorodd nor yourself will be shamed by my visits in the future.'

'That's wise of you,' said Snorri.

With that they parted. Snorri rode on to the ship, and from there back home to Helgafell.

Next day Bjorn rode south to the ship at Hraun Haven and that same summer took passage abroad. They were late putting out and ran into north-easterly gales which blew for a good part of the summer. Nothing was heard of the ship for a long time.

☘

48. TO GREENLAND

When the peace-terms between the men of Eyr and those of Alftafjord had been arranged, Snorri Thorbrandsson and his brother Thorleif Kimbi sailed to Greenland. Thorleif lived there till he was an old man, and Kimba Bay between the glaciers in Greenland is named after him. Snorri went to Vinland the Good with Karlsefni and died like a man in battle with the Skrælings.[1]

Thorodd Thorbrandsson took over the farm at Alftafjord. He married Ragnhild, daughter of Thord, son of Thorgils Eagle, son of Hallstein the Priest of Hallstein's Ness, who owned the slaves.[2]

☙

49. CHRISTIANITY IN ICELAND

The next part of the story tells how Gizur the White and his son-in-law Hjalti came to Iceland to preach the faith. Everyone in Iceland was baptized, and Christianity was adopted by law at the Althing. It was Snorri the Priest who more than anyone else persuaded the people in the Westfjords to embrace the new faith. Soon after the Assembly broke up he started building a church at Helgafell, and his father-in-law Styr another one at Hraun. The priests promised each farmer as many places in Heaven as there was standing room in any church he might build. This proved a great inducement to them to put up churches and Thorodd the Tribute-Trader had one built on his farm at Frodriver, but since there were only a few priests in Iceland at the time, it was hard to find any to sing mass in them.[1]

1. *Skræling* was the Icelandic word used to denote an indigenous inhabitant of Greenland or America: see *The Vinland Sagas*.
2. An allusion to the *Book of Settlements*, Chapter 123.

---

1. The most detailed account of Iceland's conversion to Christianity is to be found in *Kristni Saga*. See also *Njal's Saga*, pp. 216–24.

☙

50. THORGUNNA

In the summer that Christianity was adopted by law in Iceland, a ship from Dublin put in at Snæfell Ness. Most of the crew came from Ireland and the Hebrides, but there were some Norwegians too. They lay at Rif for a good part of the summer, then with a fair wind sailed up the fjord to Dogurdar Ness, where a number of people from the neighbourhood came to trade with them.

There was a Hebridean woman on board called Thorgunna, and the crew said she had some valuable things with her, difficult to get in Iceland. When Thurid of Frodriver heard about it, she was very keen to see all this finery, for she was a vain woman and extremely fond of elegant clothes and rich adornment. She travelled to the ship to see Thorgunna and asked if she had something very special in ladies' clothing. Thorgunna said she had nothing for sale, but added that she had plenty of fine things to wear herself, so that she had no need to feel ashamed to go to feasts and other gatherings. Thurid asked her to show her her things. Thorgunna did so, and Thurid thought them attractive and tastefully made, but not particularly expensive. Thurid made an offer for them, but Thorgunna refused to sell. Then Thurid invited her to come and stay with her, for she kept thinking about all the fine things she had seen, and hoping she could get them from her later on.

'Yes, I'd like to stay with you,' said Thorgunna. 'But there's something you should know. I'm not all that keen to pay cash for my board and lodging. I'm still a strong woman, and I don't mind working as long as I don't have to do heavy work. But I'll make up my own mind about how much of my money I pay out.'

Thorgunna spoke very stiffly, but that didn't prevent Thurid from urging her to come and stay with her, so Thorgunna had her baggage put ashore, a heavy trunk which she kept locked, and a lighter one, and both were taken to Frodriver. As soon as she arrived, she asked to be shown to her bed, and was given a place in the inner part of the main room. She opened the big chest and took from it a set of bedclothes, beautifully made. She spread English sheets on her bed, laid a silk-covered quilt on top, then took bed-curtains from the chest and a canopy as well. It was all so marvellous, no one could remember having ever seen anything like it.

'How much would you take for the whole set?' asked Thurid.

'I don't care how refined and ladylike you are,' said Thorgunna, 'I'm not going to sleep on bare straw just to satisfy you.'

Thurid was far from pleased about this, and it was the last time she offered to buy Thorgunna's things from her.

Thorgunna spent every day weaving, unless there was haymaking to do, and when the weather was good, she used to work at drying the hay in the home meadow. She had a special rake made for her which she let no one else touch. Thorgunna was a massive woman, tall, broad-built, and getting very stout. She had dark eyebrows and narrow eyes, and beautiful chestnut hair. Her manner was always very proper, and she used to go to Mass every morning before starting work, but she was hard to get on with and wasted little time on conversation. People thought she must be in her fifties, though she was a woman who still had a lot of life in her.

By this time Thorir Wood-Leg and his wife Thorgrima Witch-Face had come to live at Frodriver, and soon there was trouble between them and Thorgunna. Kjartan the farmer's son was the only one there Thorgunna took to, and she liked him a lot, but he kept his distance, which she found extremely irritating. Kjartan was thirteen or fourteen at the time, a big lad, and very manly.

☙

51. THORGUNNA DIES

The summer was wet, but there were good drying spells in the autumn once the home meadow at Frodriver had been mown, and nearly half of that hay was fully dry. One day was ideal for drying, calm and clear, with not a cloud in sight. Thorodd was up early that morning and arranged the work for the day. Some of the farmhands were to cart the hay home and others to stack it. He told the women to help with the drying of the hay, and shared out the work between them. Thorgunna was given as much hay to dry as would have been winter fodder for an ox.

Everything went smoothly to begin with, but in the early afternoon a black cloud began to form in the north, just above Skor, and soon it swept across the sky, making straight for the farmstead. It looked as if the cloud would bring rain, and Thorodd told them to start stacking the hay, but Thorgunna kept turning hers as hard as she could, and refused to begin stacking it even though she had been told to. The dark cloud raced across the sky, and when it was just over the farmstead at Frodriver, things were so overcast they could see nothing beyond the meadow, and hardly an arm's length inside it. After that there was such a heavy cloudburst that all the hay on the ground was drenched. The cloud vanished suddenly, and when the weather cleared up again, they saw that the shower had been one of blood.

In the evening there was a fine drying-spell, and the blood dried quickly, except on the hay that Thorgunna had spread. Neither this nor the rake she had used would dry.

Thorodd asked Thorgunna what this omen could mean, but she said she couldn't tell. 'Most likely it forebodes the death of someone here,' she said.

Thorgunna went home in the evening straight to bed. She

took off the blood-soaked clothes she was wearing, lay down on the bed and gave a heavy sigh. People could see that she had been taken ill. The shower had fallen nowhere else, only on Frodriver. Thorgunna refused food that evening. Next morning Thorodd went to see her about her illness and find out when she thought she might be feeling better. She said she believed this illness would be her last.

'I've found you to be the most sensible person here,' she said, 'and that's why I'm telling you what to do with the things I leave behind. You may not think much of me, but everything I tell you will turn out exactly as I say, and nothing good will come of it if you don't follow my wishes. This first omen is a clear indication that something serious is bound to happen unless every step is taken to prevent it.'

'You're probably not far from the truth,' said Thorodd. 'I promise to follow all your instructions.'

'Here's what I want,' said Thorgunna. 'Should I die of this illness I want my body taken to Skalholt,[1] because something tells me it will soon be the most venerated place in the land. I know there are priests there to sing Mass for me as well, and that's why I want you to take me there. In return you can have sufficient of my belongings to repay you handsomely for all your trouble, but before you start dividing up my property, Thurid is to have the scarlet cloak. I'm doing this to make her less unhappy about the disposal of the rest of my things. Next, out of all the things I'm leaving with you, take whatever you and your wife want most, to cover your expenses. There's a gold ring of mine which must be given to the church: but my bed and all its furnishings I want burnt to ashes, for they'll never do anyone much good. I'm not saying this because I grudge these things to anyone who could use them, but I must be firm about it. I wouldn't like to be responsible for all the

---

1. In 1056 Skálholt became the seat of the first native Icelandic bishop; and soon it was an important centre of learning and culture. It remained an episcopal see until the end of the eighteenth century.

trouble people will bring on themselves if they don't respect my wishes.'

Thorodd promised to do all that she asked him. Soon after, her illness took a turn for the worse and she lingered on only a few days before she died.

The body was taken to church and Thorodd had a coffin made for it. Next day he carried the bedclothes outside, gathered some firewood, and made a bonfire. When his wife Thurid came and asked what he was up to, he said he was going to burn them, just as Thorgunna had asked.

'If I have my way,' she said, 'I'm not having you burn valuable stuff like this.'

'She meant every word when she said it wouldn't do to ignore her warning,' said Thorodd.

'It only goes to show what an envious woman she was,' said Thurid. 'She was too mean to let anyone else enjoy them, and that's why she told you to do it. Whatever we decide to do, I can't see what harm can come of it.'

'I don't think ignoring her wishes will do us much good,' he said.

But Thurid put her arms round his neck and begged him not to burn the bed-furnishings. She kept pleading with him until he agreed only to destroy the eiderdown and pillows, while Thurid took the quilt, the bed-curtains, and the canopy. All the same, neither of them felt really happy about it. After that they got ready to send the corpse off for burial.

For the journey Thorodd chose men he could rely on and gave them his best horses. The corpse was wrapped in an unstitched linen shroud and laid in a coffin. They set off, taking the usual route south across the moor, and nothing much happened on their journey till they came south of Valbjarnarvellir. As they crossed the sodden moorland there, the pack-horse kept throwing off the coffin. On they went, south to the Nordur River, and crossed it at Eyjar Ford through very deep water. The weather was squally with sleet and heavy rain. Eventually they came to a farm called Nether Ness in Stafholtstungur and asked to stay the night, but the farmer refused to give them hospitality. It was getting very late, and they thought they could go no further, as it seemed unwise to risk fording the Hvit River at night, so they unloaded the horses, carried the coffin into a storehouse near the door, walked into the living-room, and took off their clothes, intending to spend the night there, without food if necessary.

The household went to bed before it grew dark. They hadn't been long in their beds when they heard loud noises coming from the larder, and some of them went to see if thieves had broken into the house. When they came to the larder, there was a tall woman, stark naked, not a stitch of clothing on her, getting a meal ready. The people of the household were too scared when they saw her to come anywhere near. As soon as the corpse-bearers heard about it, they went to see for themselves what was going on. The woman was Thorgunna, and everyone thought it best to leave her in peace. When she had finished doing what she wanted in the larder, she carried the food into the living-room, laid the table, and served the meal.

'Before we part, you may end up very sorry that you didn't treat us more hospitably,' said the corpse-bearers to the farmer.

'We'll gladly give you food and anything else you need,' said the farmer and his wife.

And as soon as the farmer had made them welcome, Thorgunna walked out of the room and didn't reappear.

Now a lamp was lit in the living-room, and the travellers were helped out of their wet clothes and given dry things. They sat down at table and made the sign of the cross over the food, and the farmer had every corner of the house sprinkled with holy water. The travellers ate their food, and it did them no harm at all, even though it had been prepared by Thorgunna. They spent a very comfortable night there.

In the morning they got ready to be on their way, and the rest of the journey went without a hitch. Everyone who heard what had happened at the first farm thought it best to give

them all that they asked for, and nothing else happened on the
journey. They came to Skalholt and handed over the precious
gifts Thorgunna had left for the church there, which the priests
accepted with pleasure. So Thorgunna was buried, and the
corpse-bearers set off home. They had an easy journey and got
back safely.

52. AN OMEN

The farm at Frodriver had a large living-room with a bed-closet
behind it, as was usual in those days. In front of the living-
room there were two store-rooms on either side of the door,
one for dried fish and the other for flour. They used to have a
great fire burning in the living-room every evening, and
people would sit beside it for hours on end before they had
their evening meal.

The evening the corpse-bearers came back, the people at
Frodriver were sitting by the fireside when they saw a half-
moon appear on the panelled wall. Everyone could see it. The
moon kept circling round the room, backing from left to right,
and stayed in sight as long as people remained at the fire.

Thorodd asked Thorir Wood-Leg what it meant, and Thorir
said it was a fatal moon. 'There'll be deaths here,' he added.

It went on like this for a whole week; every evening the same
weird moon appeared in the living-room.

❣

53. THE HAUNTINGS BEGIN

The next thing to happen was that the shepherd came home one day, badly shaken. He had little to say, but when he did speak, he was very ill-tempered. He fought shy of other people and kept muttering to himself, so everyone thought he must have been bewitched. This went on for some time. When two weeks of winter had passed, he came home one evening, went straight to bed and lay down. Next morning, when people went to see him they found him dead. He was buried at the church there, and not long afterwards massive hauntings began at the place.

One night Thorir Wood-Leg went out to the privy to ease himself, and when he was on his way back to the house, he saw the shepherd standing in front of the door. Thorir tried to get inside, but the shepherd barred his way. Thorir began walking away, but the shepherd came after him, picked him up, and threw him hard against the door. This gave Thorir a nasty shock and a good many bruises, but he struggled back to bed. Later he became ill, then died, and was buried at the church there. After that, the pair of them, Thorir Wood-Leg and the shepherd, were often seen together. As you might expect, people were terrified.

After Thorir's death, one of Thorodd's farm-hands fell ill. He lay in bed for three days, and then he died. Soon people started dying one after another, six of them in all. This was just about the beginning of Advent, but in those days people in Iceland didn't observe the fast.

The store-room was stacked so full with dried fish that the door would hardly open. The pile of fish went right up to the cross-beam, and people had to use a ladder to get at it from above. Then things started happening. Night after night, as people were sitting at the fire, they could hear something tearing at the dried fish, but when they went to look, not a living thing could they see there.

That winter, shortly before Christmas, Thorodd went out to Ness to get more dried fish for himself. There were six of them together in a ten-oared boat, and they spent the night at Ness. In the evening, after Thorodd had gone and the fire had been lit, people came into the living-room and saw a seal's head coming up through the floor. One of the servants was the first to notice this as she came in. She grabbed a club in the doorway and hit the seal on the head. Which only made it rise up out of the ground a little more. Then it turned its eyes towards the canopy from Thorgunna's bed. One of the farm-hands came up and started hitting the seal, but it kept rising further up with every blow, until its flippers emerged. At that the man fainted, and everyone was paralyzed with horror, except for young Kjartan, who rushed up with a sledge-hammer and struck the seal on the head. It was a powerful blow, but the seal only shook its head and gazed around. Kjartan went on hammering the head and driving it down like a nail into the floor till the seal disappeared, then he flattened out the floor above its head. Throughout the winter it was always the same story, Kjartan was the only one who could put fear into the ghosts.

☙

54. MORE GHOSTS

Next morning Thorodd and his men put out from Ness with their dried fish, and they were all drowned off Enni. The boat and the fish were washed ashore there, but the bodies were never found.

When the news came to Frodriver, Kjartan and Thurid invited their neighbours to a funeral feast, at which they used the Christmas ale. On the first evening of the feast, when all the guests were seated, Thorodd and his companions came

into the room drenched to the skin. Everyone welcomed
Thorodd and his men, and thought this a happy omen because
in those days it was believed that drowned people had been
well received by the sea-goddess, Ran, if they came to their
own funeral feast. At that time a good many heathen beliefs
still prevailed, though people were baptized and supposed to
be Christians. Thorodd and his men walked across the main
room, which had two doors, and into the living-room. They
ignored the greetings people gave them and sat down at the
fire. The people ran out of the living-room, but Thorodd and
his men stayed on until the fire began to burn very low, then
went away. As long as the funeral feast lasted this continued:
every evening the drowned men would come to the fire. It
gave people at the feast plenty to talk about, but some of them
thought it would stop once the feast was over.

After the feast all the guests went back home and the place
seemed rather dull without them. In the evening after the
guests had gone the fire in the living-room was lit as usual, and
as soon as it was ablaze, Thorodd and his companions came in,
all of them soaking wet. They sat down at the fire and began
squeezing the water out of their clothes. No sooner had they
taken their seats than Thorir Wood-Leg and his six companions came into the room, all of them covered with earth.
They started shaking the dirt out of their clothes and throwing
mud at Thorodd and his men. The people ran out of the room,
as you would expect, and that evening they had to do without
light, heating-stones, and everything else the fire provided.[1]
Next evening they lit a fire in another room, hoping the dead
men would not come there, but things turned out otherwise.
Everything happened just as before, and both parties came to
sit by the fire. On the third evening, Kjartan suggested they
should light a long-fire[2] in the living room, and another in a

---

1. Stones were heated by the fire and then used to warm up food and drinks.
2. *Langeldr*, a long hearth running down the centre of the main room. See
   Njal's Saga, p. 55.

separate room for the household, so they tried that. As it turned out, Thorodd and the other dead men came and sat at the long-fire, while the living sat at the smaller one, and so it continued throughout the Christmas season.

By that time the noises from the fish-pile had grown much louder, and day and night people could hear the fish being torn up. Soon the time came for the fish to be eaten, and they had a look at the pile. Someone got on top of it and saw a tail sticking out. It had the look of a singed ox-tail, but was covered with short seal-hair. The man on the stack took hold of it. First he tried to pull it out himself, then called for others to come and help him. Several people, men and women, joined him on the stack and kept pulling at the tail, but they couldn't budge it an inch. Everybody thought the tail was dead, but as they were struggling to get it out, the tail tore right through their hands, and the skin was ripped off the palms of those who had been pulling hardest. The tail was never seen again. They started clearing the fish out of the store-room, and when they got down into the pile, they saw that all the meat had been torn off the fish and only the skins left behind, but no sign of a living creature in it anywhere.

Shortly afterwards Thorgrima Witch-Face, Thorir Wood-Leg's widow, fell ill, and after a short spell in bed she died. On the very evening of her burial she was seen in her husband's company. Then the sickness that had been raging when the hairy tail had made its first appearance broke out again, this time killing more women than men. Six people died one after another, and the hauntings and night-walkings drove others away from the farm. There had been thirty servants there in the autumn, but eighteen of them died, five more ran away, and by midwinter there were only seven of them left.

☙

55. THE GHOSTS ARE BANISHED

After these weird events had been going on for some time, Kjartan set off one day over to Helgafell to see his uncle Snorri and ask his advice about what should be done to put an end to them. At that time there was a priest staying at Helgafell, sent to Snorri by Gizur the White. Snorri asked the priest to go with Kjartan to Frodriver along with his son Thord the Cat and six other people. They must burn the canopy from Thorgunna's bed, said Snorri, and then summons all the dead to a door-court. After that the priest was to sing Mass, consecrate water, and hear people's confessions. They rode over to Frodriver, and on the way there they asked the neighbours to come with them.

It was Candlemas Eve when they came to Frodriver, and the fire had just been lit. Thurid had been taken with the same illness as those who had died. Kjartan went straight into the living-room and saw Thorodd and the other dead people sitting by the fire as usual. He pulled down the canopy from Thorgunna's bed, plucked a brand from the fire, then went out and burnt to ashes all the bed-furnishings that had once belonged to Thorgunna.

Next Kjartan summonsed Thorir Wood-Leg, and Thord the Cat summonsed Thorodd for trespassing on the home and robbing people of life and health. All the dead ones at the fire were summonsed in the same way. Then the door-court was held and charges made, the proper procedure of ordinary lawcourts being observed throughout. The jury was appointed, testimony was taken, and the cases were summed up and referred for judgment. As sentence was being passed on Thorir Wood-Leg, he rose to his feet, 'I sat here as long as people would let me,' he said, then went out through the other door where the court was not being held.

After that, sentence was passed on the shepherd, and he stood up. 'I'll go now,' he said, 'and it seems I should have gone sooner.'

When Thorgrima Witch-Face heard her sentence, she stood up, too. 'I stayed as long as you let me,' she said.

So they all were sentenced one after another; and as they were sentenced, they got up, made some such remark, and left the room. It was clear that none of them wanted to go.

Thorodd was the last to be sentenced. When he heard the judgment, he stood up. 'There's no peace here,' he said, 'we'd best all be on our way.' And with that he walked out.

Then Kjartan and the others went back inside, and the priest carried holy water and sacred relics to every corner of the house. Next day he sang all the prayers and celebrated Mass with great solemnity, and there were no more dead men haunting Frodriver after that. Thurid began to improve and got well again. In the spring after all these strange events Kjartan engaged new servants. He farmed at Frodriver for a long time, and people thought him a very courageous man.

❦

56. SNORRI'S ENEMIES

Snorri the Priest lived at Helgafell for eight years after Christianity was adopted by law in Iceland. During Snorri's last year at Helgafell, his father-in-law, Styr, was killed at Jorvi in Flisuhverfi, and he travelled south to Hrossholt to fetch Styr's body. When he came into the women's room, there was Styr sitting up with his arms round the farmer's daughter.

In the spring Snorri exchanged farms with Gudrun, Osvif's-daughter, and moved house to Tongue in Sælingsdale, two

years after Gudrun's husband Bolli Thorleiksson had been
killed.[1]

That same spring Snorri and his men went south to Borgarfjord, four hundred strong, to take action over the killing of
Styr. With him were Styr's brother, Vermund the Slender,
living then at Vatnsfjord, Steinthor of Eyr, Thorodd Thorbrandsson of Alftafjord, Thorleik Brandsson of Kross Ness,
Styr's nephew, and a good many other leading men, but they
only got as far as the Hvit River to Haug's Ford across the river
from Bæ. Waiting for them on the south bank were Illugi the
Black, Kleppjarn the Old, Thorstein Gislason, Gunnlaug
Adder-Tongue, Thorstein Thorgilsson of Hafsfjord Island,
who was married to Vigdis, Illugi the Black's-daughter, and
many other notable men, more than five hundred strong.

Since Snorri and his men were barred from crossing the
river, they started proceedings when they had got as close to
the others as they thought safe. Snorri summonsed Gest for
the killing of Styr, but that summer at the Althing Thorstein
Gislason dismissed Snorri's case. In the autumn Snorri rode
south to Borgarfjord and killed Thorstein Gislason and his
son Gunnar. Along with Snorri on that expedition there
were fifteen men all told, among them Steinthor of Eyr,
Thorodd Thorbrandsson, Bard Hoskuldsson, and Thorleik
Brandsson.

Next spring Snorri the Priest and Thorstein of Hafsfjord
Island, Illugi the Black's son-in-law, met at the Thor's Ness
Assembly. Thorstein was the son of Thorgils, son of Thorfinn,
son of Sel-Thorir of Raudamel. Thorstein's mother was Aud,
daughter of Alf of the Dales, so Thorstein was cousin to
Thorgils Arason of Reykjahills, Thorgeir Havarsson, and
Thorgils Holluson, as well as to the men of Alftafjord, Thorleif
Kimbi and the other Thorbrandssons. Thorstein had prepared
a number of lawsuits for the Assembly, and one day, on the

---

1. An allusion to *Laxdæla Saga*. Gudrun egged her husband Bolli on into killing
Kjartan, his cousin and blood-brother, and later Kjartan's brothers took
revenge and killed Bolli. Snorri seems to have moved to Tongue in 1008.

slope near the court, Snorri asked Thorstein if he had many lawsuits this time. Thorstein said he had several.

'I daresay you'd like us to be as helpful to you with your cases as you and the men of Borgarfjord were to me last summer?' asked Snorri.

'No, I don't think I would,' said Thorstein.

After this, Snorri's sons and Styr's kinsmen had a good many harsh words for Thorstein, saying that it would serve him right if all his cases were dismissed and that he deserved to pay with his life for all the humiliation he and his father-in-law Illugi had caused them the previous summer. Thorstein didn't bother to answer, and people went away.

Thorstein and his kinsmen from Raudamel had many supporters, and when the court was in session he hoped to push through all the cases he had brought. Styr's kinsmen got to hear about it, and armed themselves to keep the men of Raudamel from the court by force, should they try to approach it. This led to a pitched battle between them. Thorstein of Hafsfjord Island had only one thought, to get at Snorri the Priest. Thorstein was tall and strong, and a great fighting-man, but as he was forcing his way towards Snorri, Snorri's nephew, Kjartan of Frodriver, ran to Snorri's defence. Kjartan and Thorstein attacked one another, and the fight was long and hard before friends on both sides came between them and arranged a truce.

After the battle, Snorri the Priest said to his nephew Kjartan, 'Plenty of fighting today, Breidaviking!'[2]

Kjartan was furious. 'Don't blame my background on me,' he said.

Thorstein lost seven men in the battle, and many were wounded on both sides, but the quarrel was settled on the spot at the Assembly, and Snorri's terms were very generous. He had no wish for this case to come before the Althing. No

2. An allusion to Kjartan's paternity: he was formally the son of Thorodd and Thurid, but his real father was thought to be Bjorn. See Chapter 40.

settlement had been reached over the killing of Thorstein Gislason, and he knew he would have quite enough on his hands without having to cope with yet another case.

Thormod Trefilsson described these events, the killing of Thorstein Gislason and his son Gunnar, and the Battle of the Thor's Ness Assembly, in his *Lay of the Raven*:

> Two were slain
> by the stout-hearted soldier,
> south of the stream
> rang the swords:
> seven more spirits
> slept, robbed of life,
> at Thors Ness, slaughtered
> for all to see.

It was part of their agreement that Thorstein should be free to bring all the actions he had referred to the Thor's Ness Assembly; and at the Althing that same summer, a settlement was made with regard to the killing of Thorstein Gislason and his son Gunnar. Those who had taken part with Snorri in these killings agreed to go abroad.

In the summer Thorstein of Hafsfjord Island withdrew the chieftaincy of Raudamel from the Thor's Ness Assembly as he was not pleased with the way Snorri and his supporters seemed to have got the better of him. After that Thorstein and his kinsmen set up an Assembly at Straumfjord which continued to be held for many years.[3]

3. According to the ancient Icelandic constitution, each local assembly (there were thirteen of them for the whole country) was supported by three chieftains. Nothing is known about the Straumfjord Assembly mentioned here.

57. OSPAK

Several years after Snorri had moved to Tongue in Sælings-dale, a man called Ospak was living to the north at Eyr in Bitra. Ospak was the son of Kjallak of Kjallak's River near Skridin-senni, and was married with a son called Glum, still a young man. Ospak was big and strong, but he was also a great bully, and nobody liked him. He used to go about with seven or eight men, all guilty of various offences against the farmers there in the north. Glum and his men would sail near the coast, robbing the farmers of anything they chose and stealing their driftwood.[1]

There was a man called Alf the Short at Thambardale in Bitra, who was well-off and ran a good farm. Alf was one of Snorri's supporters and looked after his driftage rights at Gudlaug's Head. Like so many other farmers, Alf had many grievances against Ospak and his men about which he would complain every time he saw Snorri.

At that time Thorir Gold-Hardarson was farming at Tongue in Bitra. He was a friend of Sturla Thjodreksson, known as Killer-Sturla, who lived at Stadarhol in Saurbæ. Thorir was a well-to-do farmer and the leading man of Bitra. He looked after Sturla's driftage rights there in the north. Ospak and Thorir were always at loggerheads, and sometimes one, then the other would come out on top. Ospak was the chief farmer in the districts of Krossardale and Enni.

One year winter set in early with heavy frost and snow, so there was no grazing in Bitra. The farmers suffered great losses in livestock, but some of them managed to get their herds

1. Driftage rights were considered a great asset to coastal farmers. Meat from stranded whales was a welcome addition to the larder, and driftwood was widely used for building.

south over the moor. The previous summer, Ospak had fortified the farmstead at Eyr, turning it into a powerful stronghold. Just after midwinter a fierce blizzard blew up from the
north, and lasted for a week. When the weather cleared,
people saw there was drift ice out in the bay, though it had not
come into the fjord at Bitra. The farmers set out to scour the
beaches for driftage, and soon the story went about that a big
finback whale had come ashore between Stika and Gudlaug's
Head. Snorri the Priest and Sturla Thjordreksson had the
greatest claim to the whale, but Alf the Short and other farmers
had a share in it too. Some of the Bitra people went with Thorir
and Alf to cut up the whale, and as they were busy carving
away at it, they saw a boat coming from Eyr across the fjord.
Soon they recognized the twelve-oared boat belonging to
Ospak. The crew beached the boat near the whale and stepped
ashore, fifteen-strong and fully armed. Ospak made straight
for the whale and asked who was in charge. Thorir said he was
looking after Sturla's share and Alf was seeing to his share and
Snorri the Priest's. 'The other farmers are taking care of their
own shares,' he added.

Ospak asked how much of the whale they were going to let
him have.

'You'll get nothing of what I'm responsible for,' said Thorir,
'but I can't speak for the other farmers. They may be willing to
sell you theirs. How much do you want to pay for it?'

'You ought to know better, Thorir,' said Ospak. 'I'm not in
the habit of buying whale-meat from you Bitra people.'

'I don't think you'll get any without paying for it,' said
Thorir.

The chunks of whale-meat already cut were piled up in a
heap, but were still to be shared out. Ospak told his men to
start loading the meat into the boat. The whale-cutters had no
weapons except for the axes with which they were cutting up
the whale, but when Thorir saw Ospak and his men making
for the whale, he urged the farmers not to stand for this
thievery, and they all rushed forward with Thorir in the lead.

Ospak turned to meet Thorir and struck him with the back of his axe. The blow landed on his ear, knocking him senseless. The men with him pulled him back and tried to bring him round, so there was nobody left to defend the whale carcass.

Then Alf the Short stepped forward and asked Ospak not to take the whale. 'You'd better keep out of this, Alf,' said Ospak, 'you have a thin skull, and I've a heavy axe. One step more, and you'll finish up worse than Thorir.' It was good advice, and Alf took it.

Ospak and his men kept on loading the whale-meat into the boat and just as they finished, Thorir came to. He saw what had happened and spoke angrily to his men for being such cowards, standing idly by while they watched people being robbed and beaten. Then he sprang to his feet, but Ospak and his men had already launched their boat and put out to sea. They rowed across the fjord over to Eyr, and started work on what they had stolen. Ospak would let no one leave who had been with him on this trip, so they all stayed on at the fortified farmstead and prepared to withstand a siege.

Thorir and the others divided up what was left of the whale, each taking his proper share of the loss, and then they went back home. Thorir and Ospak were now bitter enemies. Ospak had a lot of men with him, and soon he began to run out of provisions.

58. FIGHTING

One night Ospak set out with fourteen men over to Thambardale. They went straight into the house, herded Alf and his household into the living-room, looted the farm and carried their plunder away on four horses. The people at Fjardarhorn saw them leaving and sent someone over to Tongue to tell Thorir. Quickly he gathered some men and set out eighteen-strong for the head of the fjord, where he saw Ospak and his companions riding north from Fjardarhorn. Ospak saw the riders following them.

'There are some men over there,' he said. 'It must be Thorir out to avenge the blow I gave him earlier in the winter. There are eighteen of them against our fifteen, but we're better armed, and it's hard to say who is keener for a fight. The horses we took from Thambardale would run back home, but I'm not going to give up what I've taken. The two weakest men here had better drive them over to Eyr and tell my men to hurry and help us. The rest of us will have to stand here and fight, no matter what comes of it.' They did as they were told.

When Thorir came up with his men, Ospak greeted them and asked the news, talking very smoothly to gain time. Thorir asked where they had picked up all this loot, and Ospak said at Thambardale.

'How did you come by it?' asked Thorir.

'It wasn't given or sold,' said Ospak, 'nothing was paid for it.'

'Will you give it up and hand it over to us?' asked Thorir.

Ospak said he was not very keen to do that.

So they set on one another and fighting broke out. Thorir and his men moved hard into the attack, but Ospak's party defended strongly in spite of being outnumbered. Soon some of them were wounded and others were dead. Armed with a barbed spear, Thorir charged up to Ospak and lunged at him, but he parried the blow. Thorir had put all his strength into it, and as he missed, he went down on his knees with his head touching the ground. Ospak hewed at him with the back of his axe and there was a loud crack.

'Maybe this will teach you not to stray so far from home, Thorir,' he said.

'You could be right,' said Thorir, 'but I don't think a rap from you will stop me making all the trips I want.' He had been wearing a knife on a strap round his neck, as people used to in those days, and the knife happened to be dangling down his

back. That was where the blow had landed, so he only had a
scratch on either side.

One of Thorir's companions aimed a blow at Ospak, but as
he parried it with his axe, the sword struck the axe-handle and
broke it in two so that the axe-head fell to the ground. At that,
Ospak took to his heels and told his men to make a run for it
too. Thorir got back on to his feet and cast a spear that caught
Ospak in the thigh and went straight through. Ospak pulled
the spear out of the wound, and turned and threw it at the man
who had aimed the first blow at him, killing him instantly. As
Ospak and his companions ran off, Thorir and his men chased
them north along the beaches up to Eyr, where a number of
people, men and women, came running down from the farm,
so Thorir and his men had to turn back. There were no more
clashes between them for the rest of the winter. Three of
Ospak's men were killed in the fight and one of Thorir's, while
a good many on either side were wounded.

☙

59. MORE LOOTING

Snorri the Priest took over the case against Ospak and his men
from Alf the Short, and had them all sentenced to outlawry at
the Thor's Ness Assembly. When it was over, Snorri went back
home to Tongue and waited till it was time to hold the court of
confiscation,[1] then set off north to Bitra with a large number of
men, but found that Ospak had gone, taking all his belongings
with him. In fact Ospak had sailed off north to the Strands with
fifteen men in two boats, and there they stayed for the rest of
the summer, causing plenty of trouble. They settled down at

1. A convicted outlaw forfeited the right to own property, and a formal court
   of confiscation was supposed to be held over him at his home fourteen days
   after sentence had been passed. When the creditors had been paid what the
   outlaw owed and the chieftain had taken his fee for holding the court, the
   rest of the confiscated property was shared out between the judges and the
   farmers in the district.

Tharalatursfjord in the north, and more men began gathering round them. They were joined by one called Hrafn the Viking, a criminal who had been living as an outlaw in the North Strands. They did a lot of damage in these parts, looting and killing, and the whole gang of them stayed there till the beginning of winter. Then the men of the Strands got together, and with several other farmers Olaf Eyvindarson of Drangar led an attack on the outlaws who had fortified the farm at Tharalatursfjord and were now thirty strong. Olaf and his men laid siege to the stronghold, but it seemed quite impregnable. The farmers talked things over with the trouble-makers, who offered to leave the Strands and cause no more harm there. Since the farmers thought they were never going to gain the upper hand, they accepted the offer, and both sides swore an oath to keep the agreement. After that the farmers went back home.

☙

60. THORIR IS KILLED

As for Snorri the Priest, he set off north to Bitra to hold the court of confiscation and found that Ospak had gone away from Eyr. Snorri held the court of confiscation fully according to law, claimed the property of the outlaws, and divided it out between Alf the Short and all the other farmers who had suffered most through the outlaws' robberies. After that Snorri the Priest rode back home to Tongue.

The summer passed, and at the start of winter Ospak and his men left the North Strands in two large boats. They sailed south along the coast, then across the bay over to Vatns Ness, where they went ashore and loaded up two full cargoes of plunder. After that they sailed back west across the bay over to Bitra, put in at Eyr, and carried the loot into the fortified farmhouse. Ospak's wife and his son Glum had stayed behind with two cows.

That same night the outlaws put out again, sailed their two boats up to the head of the fjord, walked up to the farmstead at Tongue,[1] and broke into the house. They dragged Thorir out of bed, led him outside, and killed him on the spot. They rifled the house taking whatever they could lay hands on and carried everything down to the boats, then rowed over to Thambardale, rushed up to the farmstead, and broke down the door just as they had at Tongue. Alf the Short was in bed fully dressed, and when he heard the door coming down he ran out through a secret passage at the back of the house and got away into the valley.

Ospak and his men stole all they could lay hands on there and carried it down to the boats. They sailed back to Eyr fully laden, and took all the stolen property into the fortified farmhouse, then hauled the boats into the stronghold and filled them with water. They made the stronghold completely impregnable, and stayed there throughout the winter.

❦

61. ALF AND SNORRI

Alf the Short ran off south across the moor without a stop till he came to Tongue, where he told his troubles to Snorri the Priest, urging him to set out north at once and attack Ospak. However, Snorri first of all wanted to get more news from the north, find out whether Ospak had done anything more than scare Alf away, and whether he had settled down somewhere else in Bitra. A little later news came south from Bitra that Ospak had killed Thorir, and that it was going to be no easy matter to overcome him.

Snorri sent for Alf's family to come with what was left of

---

1. Tongue in Bitra, not to be confused with Tongue in Sælingsdale, where Snorri lived.

their property, and they stayed with him for the rest of the winter. Snorri's enemies criticized him for being so slow putting things right for Alf, but he let people talk, and still did nothing. Sturla Thjodreksson sent word east to Snorri that he was ready to join him any time in an attack on Ospak, saying it was just as much his duty as Snorri's.

Throughout the winter up to Christmas, reports kept coming in from the north that Ospak and his men were causing trouble. The weather was bitterly cold, with all the fjords frozen over. Just before Lent, Snorri the Priest sent a messenger west to Ingjaldshvall in Ness to a farmer there called Thrand Stigandi, son of that Ingjald who gave his name to Ingjaldshvall. Thrand was a big, strong man and a very fast runner. At one time he had been a member of Snorri's household. Thrand was said to have been a sorcerer in his heathen days, but most people gave up all their sorcery once they were baptized. Snorri sent word asking him to come east to Tongue and prepare for a dangerous mission. When the message arrived, Thrand spoke to the messenger. 'Take it easy here as long as you like,' he said. 'I shall do as Snorri tells me, but you'll never be able to keep up with me.'

The messenger said he couldn't tell till they had tried, but in the morning when he got up, Thrand had already gone and taken his weapons. Thrand walked east by Enni, then followed the usual path to Buland Head round the heads of the fjords to the farm called Eid. From there he crossed Kolgrafa Fjord, Selja Fjord, and Vigra Fjord, then up to the head of Hvamm Fjord all the way over the ice, and came to Tongue in the evening when Snorri was having his meal. He and Thrand greeted each other warmly, then Thrand asked what Snorri wanted of him and said he was ready to go anywhere, no matter what Snorri had in mind. Snorri asked him to stay the night and rest, and someone came to help Thrand off with his wet clothes.

☯

62. THE CRIMINALS ARE KILLED

That same night Snorri the Priest sent another messenger west to Stadarhol to ask Sturla Thjodreksson to come and join him the following day at Tongue north in Bitra. Snorri sent for his neighbours, too, and next day they set out fifty-strong north across Gafl Fell Moor. They came to Tongue in the evening, where Sturla was waiting for them with thirty men, and that night they went north to Eyr. When they got there, Ospak came out onto the stronghold wall and asked who was their leader. They told him who they were, and ordered the men in the stronghold to surrender. Ospak said he would never do that, 'But,' said he, 'we'll make you the same offer as we made to the men of the Strands: we'll leave the district, if you'll go away from our stronghold.' Snorri said it was not for Ospak and his men to lay down terms.

In the morning at daybreak they laid plans for the assault on the stronghold, dividing responsibilities. Snorri the Priest was to attack the side defended by Hrafn the Viking, and Sturla was to tackle Ospak's side. Sam and Thormod, the sons of Bork the Stout, were to attack the third side, and Snorri's sons Thorodd and Thorstein the Cod-Biter the fourth. Mostly Ospak and his men used stones to hold off the attack as well as they could, but they fought hard and kept up a good steady stream of missiles. Snorri and Sturla hit back at them with arrows and spears. They had a good supply, having spent time over their preparations to make sure they could take the fortress. There was fierce fighting, and a number of men on both sides were wounded, but nobody was killed. Snorri and his party kept up such a rain of missiles that Hrafn's men were forced to take cover behind the wall. Then Thrand Stigandi took a running jump and got high enough up the wall to hook his axe over the top. He climbed the shaft hand over hand and got into the stronghold. When Hrafn saw someone had got into the stronghold, he rushed at him lunging with a spear, but Thrand parried and hewed at Hrafn's shoulder severing his arm. By that time people were crowding all round him, but he jumped off the wall and managed to get back to the others.

Ospak kept urging his men to stand firm, and he himself put up a brave fight. He went right up to the wall to throw stones at Sturla and his men, but once he went too far, and the thonged spear which Sturla threw at Ospak caught him in the waist and knocked him right off the wall. Sturla rushed up and would let no one else touch him, for he wanted there to be no doubt that he was Ospak's killer. Soon a third man was killed, this time at the wall where Bork's sons were attacking.

Then the vikings surrendered, on condition they would be neither maimed nor killed. They said they would agree to any terms Snorri and Sturla wanted, and since the attackers were running out of missiles, they accepted the offer. So the men in the stronghold laid down their arms and surrendered to Snorri the Priest, and he honoured their condition that they would be neither maimed nor killed. Hrafn, Ospak, and another man were dead, and many were wounded on both sides.

This is how Thormod Trefilsson describes the battle in his *Lay of the Raven*:

> In the Battle of Bitra
> the brisk fighter gave
> hungry birds of prey
> plenty to peck at.
> Three savage vikings,
> sailors of many seas,
> lay fallen, food
> for the raven's feast.

Snorri the Priest let Ospak's widow and their son Glum keep the farm there. Later, Glum married Thordis, daughter of Asmund Grey-Lock and sister of Grettir the Strong,[1] and their

---

1. The hero of *Grettir's Saga*.

son was Ospak, who quarrelled with Odd Ofeigsson of
Midfjord.[2] Snorri the Priest and Sturla drove all these vikings
away scattering them in all directions, and once they had dealt
with them, went back home. Thrand Stigandi stayed with
Snorri the Priest for a short while, and then went home to
Ingjaldshvall. Snorri thanked Stigandi handsomely for sup-
porting him so well. Thrand Stigandi farmed for a long time at
Ingjaldshvall and later at Thrandarstad. He was a great man.

❧

63. THOROLF COMES BACK FROM
THE DEAD

Thorodd Thorbrandsson was still farming at Alftafjord and
owned the estates at Ulfarsfell and Orlygsstad as well. Thorolf
Twist-Foot's ghost haunted these farms in such a violent
fashion that no one would live there. Bolstad was now derelict,
for once Arnkel was dead, Thorolf had begun to haunt there
too, killing men and beasts alike, so that no one has ever had
the courage to farm there since. After Bolstad was abandoned,
Thorolf Twist-Foot moved on to Ulfarsfell, where he did a
great deal of damage. Everyone on the farm was terrified
whenever Thorolf Twist-Foot appeared on the scene. The
farmer at Ulfarsfell was Thorodd's tenant, so he went to
Karsstad to complain, saying everyone felt that unless something was done, Thorolf would never stop until he had cleared
the neighbourhood of men, beasts, and all. 'I can't stay there
any longer unless something is done about it,' he said.

Thorodd listened to his tenant, but was not sure how to deal
with the problem. In the morning he had his horse brought
along, told his servants to join him, and asked some of his

---

2. An allusion to *The Confederates* (*Bandamanna Saga*), one of the best shorter
   sagas.

neighbours to come too. Off they went to Twist-Foot's Knoll, where Thorolf was buried, broke open the grave, and saw Thorolf still lying there, uncorrupted with an ugly look about him. He was as black as death and swollen to the size of an ox. They tried to move the dead man, but were unable to shift him an inch. Then Thorodd put a lever under him, and that was how they managed to lift him out of the grave. After that they rolled him down to the foreshore, built a great pyre there, set fire to it, pushed Thorolf in and burnt him to ashes. Even so, it took the fire a long time to have any effect on Thorolf. A fierce gale had blown up, so as soon as the corpse began to burn the ashes were scattered everywhere, but all that they could get hold of they threw into the sea.

After that they went home, and by the time Thorodd came back to Karsstad it was getting dark. The servants were milking, and as Thorodd rode past the milking-pen, one of the cows shied away from him and stumbled, breaking her leg. They took a look at the cow and saw she was too lean for slaughtering, so Thorodd had the leg bandaged. The cow stopped yielding any milk, and when the leg had set, she was taken out for fattening to Ulfarsfell, where the pastures are as good as the best. The cow kept haunting the foreshore where they had built the funeral pyre, and she used to lick the stones where the ashes had blown about. There are people who will tell you that when the islanders came sailing up the bay with cargoes of dried fish, they used to see the cow with a dapple-grey bull up on the mountain side, but no one knew of any such bull there. Thorodd meant to put the cow down in the autumn, but when they set out to look for her, she was not to be found. Thorodd had a search made several times in the autumn, but there was no sign of her, so they all thought she must be dead or stolen.

Early one morning just before Christmas the cowherd at Karsstad went to the byre as usual. He saw a cow standing outside the door and realized it was the missing one with the broken leg. After he had led her into the byre and tied her up, he went back inside to tell Thorodd, who came to have a look at her. They saw she was with calf, so could not be put down, and Thorodd had already slaughtered enough to keep the household in meat.

Early in spring the cow gave birth to a calf, a heifer. Then a little later she bore another, this time a bull. The second delivery gave her a lot of trouble as the calf was so big, and shortly afterwards the cow died. The big calf, a dapple-grey, looked a really fine beast and they took it into the living-room. Both calves were kept there in the room, the first-born one as well.

There was an old woman at Karsstad, Thorodd's foster-mother, who had gone blind. In her younger days people used to say she had second sight, but now that she was getting on in years anything she said was just taken as an old woman's ramblings, though many of her prophecies came true. After the big calf had been tethered to the floor, it gave a loud bellow. The old woman was scared when she heard it, and said, 'That isn't a natural creature's voice, it's a monster's. You should kill the ill-omened beast.'

Thorodd said it would make no sense to slaughter such a promising calf, sure to grow into a splendid bull if reared. Then the calf bellowed a second time. The old woman started shaking and shivering. 'Do it for me, foster-son,' she said, 'kill this calf, we'll all suffer horribly if you let it live.'

'Since you want it so badly, foster-mother,' said Thorodd, 'we'll put the calf down.'

Both calves were then taken out. Thorodd had the heifer slaughtered and the bull-calf taken into the barn, but he gave strict instructions that no one should tell the old woman the big calf was still alive. Every day the calf grew bigger and bigger, so that later in the spring, when the calves were put out to graze, it was already the size of those born at the start of winter. The moment it was freed the calf started racing all over the home meadow bellowing as loudly as an old bull, and the people inside heard it clearly. 'So the monster calf hasn't been destroyed yet,' said the old woman. 'We'll suffer a worse calamity through him than any of you can imagine.'

The calf went on growing, and grazed in the home meadow all summer. By autumn it had grown bigger than any yearling bull, a fine-looking beast with magnificent horns. They called it Glæsir. In two years it had grown to the size of a five-year-old ox. It was always kept near the farm with the milch cows, and every time Thorodd came to the milking-pen, Glæsir would come up to him, sniff him and lick his clothing, and Thorodd would stroke the bull. Glæsir was as gentle as a lamb to man and beast, but whenever he bellowed the sound was terrifying. The old woman was scared out of her wits whenever she heard it.

When Glæsir was four years old, he would not let himself be driven by women, children or youngsters, and even when grown men came near, he used to raise his head and seemed ready to go for them, though if they persisted he would just give in and walk away.

One day Glæsir came to the milking-pen and bellowed so loud, people in the house thought he was standing next to them. Thorodd and the old woman were in the living-room and she gave a heavy sigh. 'You still take no notice of my warning to have the bull destroyed, foster-son,' she said.

'Cheer up, foster-mother,' said Thorodd. 'Glæsir's only to live till autumn. Once he's been fattened over summer we'll kill him.'

'That will be too late,' she said.

'I don't see what you mean,' said Thorodd.

While they were arguing about it, the bull let out an even more fearsome bellow than usual, and the old woman made this verse:

> The bull's head brawls
> and bellows an omen,
> some human he'll kill
> says my hoary old head:

> soon he'll guide you
> to the grave-scarred ground,
> bind your body
> in the bondage of death.

'You're a stupid old crone,' said Thorodd, 'you can't see anything of the sort.' She said:

> You say I'm stupid
> whenever I speak,
> but I see your body
> bloodstained and butchered:
> the bull will bellow
> and be your bane,
> this keen-eyed crone
> sees all too clearly.

'Foster-mother,' he said, 'it will never happen.'
'Unhappily it will,' she replied.

In the summer, after Thorodd's hay from the home meadow had all been gathered into large stacks, heavy rain began to fall. When the people came out next morning they saw that Glæsir was back in the meadow, and that he had thrown off the wooden block fastened to his horns when he got too lively. The bull was quite unlike his normal self. He had never interfered with the hay before when he was grazing in the meadow, but now he kept going for the stacks, driving his horns under them, tossing them into the air, and scattering the hay all over the field. As soon as he had destroyed one, he set on the next, raging and bellowing all over the meadow. The men were so scared of him that no one dared go and drive him from the hay. When Thorodd heard what Glæsir was up to, he rushed out of the house and grabbed a great birch log from the pile of firewood beside the door. Gripping it by the branches, he threw it over his shoulder and ran down the meadow towards the bull. When the bull saw him coming, it turned to face him. Thorodd lifted up the log and struck the bull such a blow between the horns the log split near the branches. At this

Glæsir flew into a rage and went for Thorodd, but he gripped it by the horns and tried to swing it round. So it went on for some time, the bull charging and Thorodd retreating and pushing it to left and right. After a while Thorodd grew tired of this and jumped on to the bull's neck. With his arms clasped round its throat, he lay there between its horns hoping to wear it down, but the bull still kept racing to and fro all over the meadow with Thorodd on its back.

Thorodd's farm-hands watched the struggle and saw how dangerous things were looking, but they did not feel confident enough to go to his rescue unarmed. So they went inside to get their weapons, then rushed out again with spears and other things, down to the meadow. When the bull saw them coming it put its head between its legs and with a sharp twist managed to get one horn right under Thorodd, then jerked its head so hard that Thorodd was thrown head over heels into the air and landed on the bull's neck. As Thorodd came down, Glæsir gave another jerk of the head and one of its horns caught Thorodd right in the belly deep into his stomach, forcing him to let go. Then Glæsir gave a loud and terrible roar and raced off across the meadow down to the river. Thorodd's men ran after the bull and chased it across Geirvör scree until they came to a quagmire just below the farmstead at Hellur. The bull charged headlong in and sank down, never to reappear. The place has been called Glæsiskelda ever since.[1]

When the men came back to the meadow, Thorodd had gone up to the house, and there in his bed they found him lying. He was dead. They carried him to church to be buried, and his son Kar took over the farm at Alftafjord. Kar lived there a long time and the farm at Karsstad takes its name from him.

---

1. Literally, 'Glæsir's swamp'.

§

64. IN THE NEW WORLD

There was a man called Gudleif, the son of Gudlaug the Wealthy of Straumfjord and brother of Thorfinn from whom the Sturlungs are descended.[1] Gudleif was a great seafaring trader and owned a large cargo ship. He and another ship-owner, Thorolf Eyra-Loftsson, fought against Earl Sigvaldi's son, Gyrd, who lost an eye in the battle.

Towards the end of St Olaf's reign[2] Gudleif set out west to Dublin on a trading voyage, intending to sail on from there to Iceland, but west of Ireland he ran into easterly, then north-easterly gales, and the ship was driven out to sea first west and then south-west, well out of sight of land. This was late in the summer, and they kept making vows to do all sorts of things if they could get back to land. At last, land came into view. It seemed a large place but they had no idea what country it was. Gudleif and his crew decided to put in, not wanting to battle against the sea any longer. They found a safe harbour, and after a while some people came down to meet them. They did not know who the inhabitants were, but they seemed to be speaking Irish. Soon a great crowd gathered there, hundreds of them, attacked the crew, took them all prisoner, shackled them, and marched them some distance inland, where they were taken to a court to be tried and sentenced. Gudleif and his men understood that some of the people wanted to put

1. The Sturlungs were the thirteenth-century descendants of Sturla Thordar-son (d. 1183: see also p. 165), particularly his sons Snorri (1179–1241), author of *The Prose Edda* and *Heimskringla*, Sighvat (d. 1238), and Thord (d. 1237), father of Sturla (1214–84), who wrote *King Hakon's Saga, King Magnus's Saga*, and *Islendingasaga* ('the Saga of Icelanders') which deals with the period *c.*1200–1262. Sturla was also the redactor of the earliest extant version of the *Book of Settlements*. The Sturlungs were one of the most powerful families in Iceland from *c.*1200 to 1262.
2. St Olaf was ruler of Norway 1015–30.

them to death, while others proposed to share them out as slaves.

The people were still arguing about it when Gudleif and his men saw a group of horsemen coming up with a banner ahead of them. It looked as if one of these must be a chieftain, and as they came closer, the Icelanders saw that the one behind the banner was an old man with a head of grey hair but tall and brave-looking. Everyone bowed to him and greeted him as their leader, and the Icelanders saw that every decision was left to him. After a while he sent for Gudleif and his crew. When they came before him he spoke to them in Icelandic and asked where they came from. They said most of them were from Iceland. When he asked which of them were Icelanders, Gudleif stepped forward and greeted him. The man gave a friendly reply and asked what part of Iceland he belonged to. Gudleif said he came from Borgarfjord, and the man asked which part of the district. Soon he began asking detailed questions about all the leading people in Borgarfjord and Breidafjord, then about Snorri the Priest and his sister Thurid of Frodriver. He followed this by asking about every member of the household at Frodriver, particularly young Kjartan, who was now farming there, but the natives started to shout that something must be done about the crew, so the tall man moved away from the Icelanders and called twelve of his own people to come and talk with him, and they had a long consultation. Eventually they returned to the meeting, and the tall man spoke to Gudleif.

'My fellow-countrymen and I have taken some time to consider your case,' he said, 'and they have left it to me to decide what should be done with you. I'm giving you leave to go wherever you want, and though you may think it's late in the summer to put out to sea, I strongly advise you to get well away from here. These people are treacherous and hard to deal with, and they think you've broken their laws.'

'What shall we tell people if we get back to our homeland?' asked Gudleif. 'Who shall we say we owe our freedom to?'

'That's one thing I'm not going to tell you,' said the man. 'I'm too fond of my kinsmen and blood-brothers to let them come here and get into the same trouble as you'd have been in had I not been here to help you. I've lived so many years, I expect old age will get the better of me any moment now, and even if I survive a little longer, there are still people here more powerful than me, and they'd not show any mercy to strangers. But it so happens that just now they're not around.'

The old man had their ship made ready and stayed with them until they got a favourable wind to take them out to sea. Before he and Gudleif parted, he took a gold ring from his finger and gave it to Gudleif along with a fine sword. Then he said, 'If you're lucky enough to get back to your homeland, give this sword to Kjartan the farmer at Frodriver, and the ring to his mother Thurid.'

'What shall I tell them,' asked Gudleif, 'about the man who sent them these gifts?'

'Tell them that he's a closer friend to the housewife at Frodriver than to her brother the chieftain at Helgafell. And should someone guess from this message who gave these precious gifts, tell him that I forbid anybody to come and look for me, because no one could make the voyage to this particular spot unless he had your luck. This is a big country and the harbours are few and far between. Strangers can expect plenty of trouble here unless they happen to be as lucky as you.'

With that they parted. Gudleif and his crew put out to sea and reached Ireland in the autumn. They spent the winter in Dublin and sailed the following summer to Iceland. Gudleif handed over the gifts, and people believe this man must have been Bjorn the Breidavik-Champion, though their only evidence is the story we've just told.

❦

65. SNORRI'S DESCENDANTS

Snorri the Priest farmed at Tongue for twenty years and had more than enough trouble on his hands while such powerful men as Thorstein Kuggason, Thorgils Holluson, and other dangerous enemies were still alive. Snorri plays a part in other sagas as well. Many people know about his role in *Laxdæla Saga*, where he was such a great friend of Gudrun, Osvif's-daughter, and her sons. Snorri figures in *Heidarviga Saga* too, for apart from Gudmund the Powerful, he was the one who gave greatest help to Bardi after the battle on the moor. The older Snorri grew, the better people came to like him, not only because his enemies were getting fewer and fewer, but also because he entered into marriage alliances with leading people in Breidafjord and elsewhere, and that increased his popularity.

Snorri married his daughter Sigrid to Brand Vermundsson the Generous, but afterwards she married Kolli, son of Thormod Thorlaksson of Eyr. Brand and Sigrid lived at Bjorn's Haven. Snorri married his daughter Unn to Killer-Bardi, but later she married Sigurd Thorisson of Bjark Isle in Norway, and their daughter was Rannveig, who married Jon, son of Arni, son of Arni Armodsson. The son of Rannveig and Jon was Vidkunn of Bjark Isle, one of the noblest of all the landed men in Norway. Snorri married his daughter Thordis to Bolli Bollason, and the Gilsbakki people are descended from them. Snorri married his daughter Hallbera to Thord, son of Sturla Thjodreksson, and their daughter was Thurid, wife of Haflidi Masson. They had a great many descendants. Snorri married his daughter Thora to Cart-Bersi, son of Halldor Olafsson of Hjardarholt, but later she married Thorgrim the Singed and a great and noble line descends from them. All the remaining daughters of Snorri were married after his death: Thurid the

Wise married Gunnlaug, son of Steinthor of Eyr; Gudrun, Snorri's-daughter, married Kolfinn of Solheimar; Halldora, Snorri's-daughter, married Thorgeir of Asgardshills; and Alof, Snorri's-daughter, married Jorund Thorfinnsson, brother of Gunnlaug of Straumfjord.

Halldor[1] was the greatest of all Snorri's sons. He lived at Hjardarholt in Laxardale, and from him the Sturlungs and the Vatnsfjord people are descended. Thorodd was the second greatest. He lived at Spakonufell in Skaga Strand. Mani Snorrason lived at Saudafell. His son Ljot was nicknamed Mana-Ljot and was considered the greatest of all Snorri's grandsons. Thorstein Snorrason lived at Laugarbrekka, and from him are descended the Asbirnings in Skagafjord and many other people besides. Thord Cat Snorrason lived at Dufgusdale; Eyjolf Snorrason lived at Lambastad in Myrar; Thorleif Snorrason lived in Medalfell Strand, and from him the Ball River people are descended; and Snorri Snorrason lived at Sælingsdale Tongue after his father. Snorri the Priest also had a son called Klepp, but no one knows where he lived, and we have no record of his descendants, if indeed he had any.

Snorri the Priest died at Tongue in Sælingsdale a year after the killing of King Olaf the Saint, and was buried at the church he himself had built. When the graveyard there was changed, his bones were removed to the site of the present church. Gudny, Bodvar's-daughter, was present, the mother of the Sturlusons, Snorri, Thord, and Sighvat, and she said that Snorri the Priest's bones were those of a man of average height, not very tall. She also said that the bones of Snorri's uncle, Bork the Stout, had been dug up, and that they were exceptionally big. The bones of old Thordis, Sur's-daughter, were dug up too, and Gudny said they were those of a small woman, and black as if they had been singed. All these

1. For an interesting story about Halldor, see *Hrafnkel's Saga and Other Icelandic Stories* (Penguin Classics, 1971), pp. 109–20.

☙

GLOSSARY OF PERSONAL NAMES

Names of characters who are only mentioned in passing are not included. Reference is made not to pages, but to chapters.

Alf the Short of Thambardale: looks after Snorri's driftage rights, 57; his farm plundered by Ospak, 58; 59; robbed again by Ospak, 60; 61.

Alfgeir, a Hebridean captain: comes to stay with Thorarin the Black at Mavahlid and fights on his side, 18; 19; 21; goes with him from Norway to the British Isles, 25.

Ari Thorgilsson the Learned, Iceland's first historian (1068–1148), 7.

Arnbjorn the Strong, brother of Bjorn the Breidavik-Champion, 15; goes abroad in search of his brother, strikes Thorleif Kimbi, 39; comes back to Iceland with Bjorn, 40; starts farming at Bakki, 40; at the ball-games, 43.

Arngrim Thorgrimsson: *see* Styr Thorgrimsson.

Arnkel the Priest, son of Thorolf Twist-Foot, 8; a temple-priest at Bolsted, 12; defends his sister Geirrid in court, 16; gives shelter to Thorarin the Black, 19; goes with Thorarin to Holt to execute Katla and Odd, 20; helps Thorarin, 21; 22; 24; advises Vermund about the berserks, 25; reluctant to take action after the killing of Vigfus, 26; yields to pressure and takes on the case, 27; trouble with his father, 30; has his father's slaves put to death for arson, 31; has Ulfar's killer put to death, 32; refuses to quarrel with Snorri, 33; re-buries his father, 34; quarrels with Snorri, 35; an attempt on Arnkel's life, 36; killed; description; burial, 37; action over his killing, 38; 63.

Asbrand of Kamb, father of Bjorn the Breidavik-Champion and others, 15; 22; binds his son's wounds, 29; 39.

Asdis Styr's-daughter, 18; Halli the berserk falls in love with her before she is married to Snorri the Priest, 28.

Asgeir Vestarsson of Eyr, 7; supports Thorgrim Kjallaksson, 9; grand-father of the Men of Eyr (q.v.), 12.

Aslak of Langadale: intervenes in the conflict between the Kjalleklings and the Thorsnessings, 9; intervenes in the Battle of Alftafjord, 44.

Aud, wife of Thorarin the Black, 15; her hand is cut off in the skirmish at Mavahlid, 18; 19; 20.

Ketilsson, 3; settles in Iceland, 6; marries Osk and has Thorstein Surt by her, 7; 48.

Harald Fine-Hair, King of Norway: fights his way to power, 1; outlaws Bjorn Ketilsson, 2.

Hrafn the Viking, a criminal: joins up with Ospak, 59; killed, 62.

Hrolf of Mostur Island: see Thorolf Mostur-Beard.

Illugi the Black, of Gilsbakki: quarrels with the Kjalleklings, 17; 56.

Katla of Holt, the widowed mother of Odd: teases Gunnlaug about Geirrid, 15; wants him to stay the night, 16; executed, 20.

Ketil Flat-Nose, a chieftain in Norway: conquers the Hebrides, marries off his daughters, 1; dies, 5.

Kjallak the Old, of Bjorn's Haven, son of Bjorn the Easterner: eponymous ancestor of the Kjalleklings (q.v.), 7.

Kjalleklings, the: 7; 9; 10; 17; 26; 27.

Kjartan Thoroddsson, of Frodriver, nephew to Snorri: birth, 29; paternity in question, 40; Thorgunna has a crush on him, 50; attacks the mysterious seal, 53; invites people to his father's funeral feast, 54; consults his uncle Snorri about the hauntings, 55; his paternity again, 56; Bjorn sends him a sword from a faraway land, 64.

Leiknir, a berserk: brought to Iceland by Vermund, 25; killed, 28.

Mar Hallvardsson, uncle to Snorri: 11, becomes overseer at Helgafell, 15; wounds Bjorn, 23; mistaken for Snorri and wounded, 24; 27; Battle of Alfta Fjord, 44; 46; 47.

Men of Alftafjord: 9; 43; 48; 56.

Men of Eyr (Eyrbyggjar): 25; 44; 45; 48.

Odd Katlason, of Holt: description, 15; claims that Geirrid bewitched Gunnlaug, 16; in the fight at Mavahlid, 18; executed, 20.

Olaf Eyvindarson, of Drangar: leads an attack on Ospak, 59.

Orlyg of Orlygsstad, a freedman: buys land from Thorolf Twist-Foot, 8; dies, 32.

Ospak Kjallaksson, a farmer in Bitra: starts plundering, 57; loots Alf the Short's farm, 58; sentenced to outlawry, 59; kills Thorir, 60; makes more trouble, 61; killed, 62.

Snorri Thorbrandsson, of Alftafjord: family background, 12; Battle of Vigra Fjord, 45; emigrates to Greenland, killed in Vinland, 48.

Snorri Thorgrimsson the Priest, posthumous son of Thorgrim the Priest, called after his father: later his name is changed to Snorri, 12; goes abroad at the age of fourteen, 13; wins Helgafell, 14; description, 15;

defends the sacred ground at Thor's Ness against the Kjalleklings, 9; 10; drowns, 11; his sons, 12.

Thorstein Cod-Biter, son of Snorri the Priest: with his father in the attack on Ospak, 62; 65.

Thorstein Thorgilsson, of Hafsfjord Island: opposes Snorri, 56.

Thorstein Hallsteinsson Surt: fostered by Thorolf Mostur-Beard, 7; given a farm on Thor's Ness by Thorstein Cod-Biter, 11.

Thrand Stigandi, of Ingjaldshvall: joins Snorri the Priest, 61; kills Hrafn the Viking, 62.

Thurid Bork's-daughter, half-sister to Snorri the Priest: marries Thorbjorn the Stout of Frodriver, 15; sends for her husband's body, 18; rumours about her and Bjorn the Breidavik-Champion, 22; marries Thorodd the Tribute-Trader and settles at Frodriver; more visits from Bjorn, 29; Bjorn calls on her, 40; 47; invites Thorgunna to stay, 50; grabs Thorgunna's bed-furnishings after her death, 51; holds a funeral feast for her second husband, 54; dies, 55; 64.

Ulfar of Ulfarsfell, a freedman: buys land from Thorolf Twist-Foot, 8, his hay stolen by Thorolf, 30; makes over his property to Arnkel, 31; killed, 32.

Ulfar the Champion, a settler: makes his home at Ulfar's Fell, 7; killed by Thorolf Twist-Foot in duel, 8.

Vermund the Slender Thorgrimsson, of Bjorn's Haven: family background, 12; inherits from his father; his wife and children, 18; supports Thorarin, 19–20; 21; brings two berserks to Iceland, 25; reluctant to take action over the killing of Vigfus, 27; arbitrates, 31; Battle of Alfta Fjord, 44; Snorri's expedition to Borgarfjord, 56.

Vigfus Bjarnarson, of Drapuhlid: family background, 7; marries Thorgerd, 8; defeated in a court case by Snorri the Priest, 23; his hired assassin fails to kill Snorri, who kills Vigfus himself, action over his killing, 27.

❧

BIBLIOGRAPHICAL NOTES

EYRBYGGJA SAGA

Manuscripts

The manuscripts of *Eyrbyggja Saga* can be divided into three groups, as
follows: (a) The *Vatnshyrna* text, represented by two seventeenth-
century transcripts of a late fourteenth-century vellum codex, now
lost: AM 448, 4to, and AM 442, 4to. (b) The so-called B-group
represented by a fourteenth-century vellum MS, preserved in Wol-
fenbüttel (see below); a fragment dating from the end of the thirteenth century: AM 162 E fol.; and a paper transcript: AM 446, 4to.
(c) The *Melabók* text, represented by an early fifteenth-century fragment: AM 445 B, 4to; and paper transcripts: AM 445 A, 4to; Lbs 982,
4to; and 1489, 4to. The edition on which the present translation is
based follows the *Vatnshyrna* text most of the way. A critical edition of
Eyrbyggja Saga, based on all known MSS, is now being prepared by
Forrest S. Scott.

Editions

Thorkelin, G. J., (editor and translator), *Eyrbyggja-saga sive Eyranorum
    historia . . .* (Copenhagen, 1787).
Vigfússon, Guðbrandr, (editor), *Eyrbyggja saga* (Leipzig, 1864).
Gering, Hugo, (editor), *Eyrbyggja saga* (Halle, Saale, 1897).
Sveinsson, Einar Olafur (editor), *Eyrbyggja saga . . .* Islenzk Fornrit 4
    (Reykjavík, 1935).
Helgason, Jón, (editor), *The Saga Manuscript 9. 10. Aug. 4to in the
    Herzog August Library Wolfenbüttel*, Manuscripta Islandica III
    (Copenhagen, 1956). Facsimile edition.

Translations

Scott, Sir Walter, 'Abstract of the Eyrbyggja-Saga', in M. Mallet
    (editor), *Illustrations of Northern Antiquities from the earlier Teutonic*

and Scandinavian Romances (Edinburgh, 1814). Based on Thorkelin's Latin version, see above.

Morris, William, and Magnússon, Eiríkr, (translators), *The Story of the Ere-Dwellers (Eyrbyggja saga)*, The Saga Library II (London, 1892).

Vigfússon, Guðbrandr, and Powell, F. V., (editors and translators), *The Thorsness Settlement – Eyrbyggja saga – The Tale of Beorn the Broadwickmen's champion* in their Origines Islandicæ I and II (Oxford, 1905).

Schach, Paul, and Hollander, Lee M., (translators), *Eyrbyggja Saga* (Lincoln, Nebraska, 1959).

Critical Works

The items below are selected from a large number of articles and notes which have appeared in print and deal with various aspects of *Eyrbyggja Saga*. For more detailed bibliographical information see Halldór Hermannsson, *Islandica* I and 24; Jóhann S. Hannesson, *Islandica* 38; and Hans Bekker-Nielsen, *A Bibliography of Old Norse-Icelandic Studies* (1963–in progress).

Boyer, Régis, Introduction to his French translation of the saga: *La Saga de Snorri le Godi* (Eyrbyggja Saga) (Paris, 1973).

Garmonsway, G. N., 'Eyrbyggja Saga', *Saga-Book of the Viking Society* xii (1940), 81–92.

Harris, Joseph, 'The Masterbuilder Tale in Snorri's *Edda* and Two Sagas', *Arkiv för nordisk filologi* xci (1976), 66–101.

Heller, Rolf, 'Das Alter der Eyrbyggja Saga im Licht der Sprachstatistik', *Acta Philologica Scandinavica* xxxii (1978), 53–66.

Hollander, Lee M., 'The Structure of Eyrbyggja Saga', *Journal of English and Germanic Philology* 58 (1959), 222–7.

Mabire, Jean-Pierre, *La composition de la Eyrbyggja Saga* (Caen, 1971).

McCreish, Bernadine, 'Structural Patterns in the *Eyrbyggja saga* and other sagas of the Conversion', *Medieval Scandinavia* 11 (1978–9; published 1982), 271–80.

McTurk, Rory, 'Approaches to the Structure of Eyrbyggja saga', *Sagnaskemmtun: Studies in honour of Hermann Pálsson*, edited by Rudolf Simek and others (Vienna, 1986), 223–7.

Ottósson, Kjartan G., *Fróðárundur í Eyrbyggju* (with a summary in English), Studia Islandica 42 (Reykjavík, 1983). Deals with the marvels at Fordriver, chapters 50–5.

Eyrbyggja Saga

Poole, Russell, 'The Origins of the *Máhlíðingavísur*', *Scandinavian Studies* 57 (1985), 274–8. Deals with the verses in chapters 18 and 19.

Schach, Paul, 'Some observations on the Helgafell episode in *Eyrbyggja saga* and *Gísla saga*' in *saga og språk. Studies in language and literature*, edited by John M. Weinstock, (Austin, Texas, 1972), 113–45.

Scott, Forrest S., 'The Icelandic family saga as precursor of the novel, with special reference to *Eyrbyggja Saga*', *Parergon* vi (1973), 3–13.

Simpson, John M., 'Eyrbyggja Saga and nineteenth-century scholarship', *Proceedings of the First International Saga Conference, Edinburgh, 1971* (London, 1973).

Tassin, Guy, 'Recherches sur la famille dans l'Eyrbyggja Saga: l'établissement des réseaux d'alliances', *Inter-Nord* xv (1979), 79–98.

OTHER SAGAS IN TRANSLATION

BANDAMANNA SAGA: in *The Confederates and Hen-Thorir*, translated by Hermann Pálsson (Edinburgh, 1975).

DROPLAUGARSONA SAGA in *Three Icelandic Sagas*, translated by M. H. Scargill and Margaret Schlauch (New York, 1950).

EGILS SAGA: *Egil's Saga*, translated by Hermann Pálsson and Paul Edwards (Harmondsworth, 1976).

EIRÍKS SAGA RAUÐA: *The Vinland Sagas*, translated by Magnus Magnusson and Hermann Pálsson (Harmondsworth and New York, 1965).

GÍSLA SAGA SÚRSSONAR: *The Saga of Gisli*, translated by George Johnston (London, 1965).

GRETTIS SAGA: *Grettir's Saga*, translated by Denton Fox and Hermann Pálsson (Toronto, 1974).

GRŒNLENDIGA SAGA: in *The Vinland Sagas*, see above.

HALLDÓRS ÞÁTTR SNORRASONAR: *Hrafnkel's Saga and other Icelandic stories*, translated by Hermann Pálsson (Harmondsworth, 1971).

HEIMSKRINGLA, translated by Lee M. Hollander (Austin, Texas, 1944).

HÆNSA-ÞÓRIS SAGA: in *The Confederates and Hen-Thorir*, see above.

JÓMSVÍKINGA SAGA: *The Saga of the Jómsvíkings*, edited and translated by N. F. Blake (Edinburgh, 1962).

LANDNÁMABÓK: *The Book of Settlements*, translated by Hermann Pálsson and Paul Edwards (Winnipeg, 1972).

LAXDÆLA SAGA, translated by Magnus Magnusson and Hermann Pálsson (Harmondsworth, 1969).

NJÁLS SAGA *Njal's Saga*, translated by Magnus Magnusson and Hermann Pálsson (Harmondsworth, 1960).

ORKNEYINGA SAGA, translated by Hermann Pálsson and Paul Edwards (Harmondsworth, 1978).

VÍGA-GLUMS SAGA, translated by John McKinnell (Edinburgh), 1987).

GENERAL WORKS

Andersson, Theodore M., *The Problem of Icelandic Saga Origins* (New Haven and London, 1964).
  The Icelandic Family Saga. An Analytic Reading (Cambridge, Massachusetts, 1967).
Hallberg, Peter, *The Icelandic Saga* translated by Paul Schach (Lincoln, Nebraska, 1962).
Jóhannesson, Jón, *A History of the Old Icelandic Commonwealth*, translated by Haraldur Bessason (Winnipeg, 1974).
Ker, W. P., *Epic and Romance. Essays on Medieval Literature* (London, 1908).
Magnusson, Magnus, *Iceland Saga* (London, 1987).
Phillpotts, Bertha, *Edda and Saga* (London, 1931).
Sveinsson, Einar Olafur, *Dating the Icelandic Sagas* (London, 1958).
Turville-Petre, G., *Origins of Icelandic Literature* (Oxford, 1953).

Western Fjords

Hunafloi Fjord

Dyra Fjord

Barda Strand

Skaga Fjord

Spakonufell

Breida Fjord   *Bitra Fjord*   East Fjords

ICELAND

Hvita

Snæfellsness   Thingvellir (Althing)

Borgar Fjord   *Horna Fjord*

Reykjaness   Skalholt

BREI

Bjarnarha

Ondurda Eyr   Borgarh

Buland Head   Hr

Krossness

Ness   Rif

Ingjaldshval   Mavahlid

Holt

Thrandarstad   Frodriver   *Salteyrar Mouth*

Arnarhval   *Hrauns Fjord*

Egilsskard

Kamb   Bakki

Oxl

Hofgardar

Laugarbrekka   *Breidavik*   *Hraunhaven*

SNÆFELLSNESS

ORD

Sælingsdale

Tongue •

Hvamm •

Kjallaksstad

Dogurdarness • •Tongue

Medalfell Strand

Thor's Ness

Vigra Fjord

Hvamms Fjord

Helgafell

•Hofstad

Langadale •Breidabolstad

•Eyr Krakuness

Dritsker Borgardale Skoga Strand

•Karstad

Holar
Hvamm •Orlygsstad

Alfta Fjord Ulfarsfell
Bolstad

orgarholt •Hrossholt

Straum Fjord

Hafsfjord Island

0   5   10

Miles

READ MORE IN PENGUIN

In every corner of the world, on every subject under the sun, Penguin represents quality and variety – the very best in publishing today.

For complete information about books available from Penguin – including Puffins, Penguin Classics and Arkana – and how to order them, write to us at the appropriate address below. Please note that for copyright reasons the selection of books varies from country to country.

In the United Kingdom: Please write to *Dept. EP, Penguin Books Ltd, Bath Road, Harmondsworth, West Drayton, Middlesex UB7 0DA*

In the United States: Please write to *Consumer Services, Penguin Putnam Inc., 405 Murray Hill Parkway, East Rutherford, New Jersey 07073-2136.* VISA and MasterCard holders call 1-800-631-8571 to order Penguin titles

In Canada: Please write to *Penguin Books Canada Ltd, 10 Alcorn Avenue, Suite 300, Toronto, Ontario M4V 3B2*

In Australia: Please write to *Penguin Books Australia Ltd, 487 Maroondah Highway, Ringwood, Victoria 3134*

In New Zealand: Please write to *Penguin Books (NZ) Ltd, Private Bag 102902, North Shore Mail Centre, Auckland 10*

In India: Please write to *Penguin Books India Pvt Ltd, 11 Community Centre, Panchsheel Park, New Delhi 110017*

In the Netherlands: Please write to *Penguin Books Netherlands bv, Postbus 3507, NL-1001 AH Amsterdam*

In Germany: Please write to *Penguin Books Deutschland GmbH, Metzlerstrasse 26, 60594 Frankfurt am Main*

In Spain: Please write to *Penguin Books S. A., Bravo Murillo 19, 1°B, 28015 Madrid*

In Italy: Please write to *Penguin Italia s.r.l., Via Vittorio Emanuele 45Ia, 20094 Corsico, Milano*

In France: Please write to *Penguin France, 12, Rue Prosper Ferradou, 31700 Blagnac*

In Japan: Please write to *Penguin Books Japan Ltd, Iidabashi KM-Bldg, 2-23-9 Koraku, Bunkyo-Ku, Tokyo 112-0004*

In South Africa: Please write to *Penguin Books South Africa (Pty) Ltd, P.O. Box 751093, Gardenview, 2047 Johannesburg*

READ MORE IN PENGUIN

A CHOICE OF CLASSICS

The Brothers Karamazov Fyodor Dostoyevsky

A drama of parricide and intense family rivalry, *The Brothers Karamazov* is Dostoyevsky's acknowledged masterpiece. It tells the story of the murder of a depraved landowner and the ensuing investigation and trial.

Selections from the Carmina Burana
A verse translation by David Parlett

The famous songs from the *Carmina Burana* (made into an oratorio by Carl Orff) tell of lecherous monks and corrupt clerics, drinkers and gamblers, and the fleeting pleasures of youth.

Fear and Trembling Søren Kierkegaard

A profound meditation on the nature of faith and submission to God's will, which examines with startling originality the story of Abraham and Isaac.

Selected Prose Charles Lamb

Lamb's famous essays (under the strange pseudonym of Elia) on anything and everything have long been celebrated for their apparently innocent charm. This major new edition allows readers to discover the darker and more interesting aspects of Lamb.

The Picture of Dorian Gray Oscar Wilde

Wilde's superb and macabre novel, one of his supreme works, is reprinted here with a masterly Introduction and valuable Notes by Peter Ackroyd.

Frankenstein Mary Shelley

In recounting this chilling tragedy Mary Shelley demonstrates both the corruption of an innocent creature by an immoral society and the dangers of playing God with science.

READ MORE IN PENGUIN

A CHOICE OF CLASSICS

ANTHOLOGIES AND ANONYMOUS WORKS

The Age of Bede
Alfred the Great
Beowulf
A Celtic Miscellany
The Cloud of Unknowing and Other Works
The Death of King Arthur
The Earliest English Poems
Early Irish Myths and Sagas
Egil's Saga
English Mystery Plays
Eyrbyggja Saga
Hrafnkel's Saga
The Letters of Abelard and Heloise
Medieval English Verse
Njal's Saga
Roman Poets of the Early Empire
Seven Viking Romances
Sir Gawain and the Green Knight

READ MORE IN PENGUIN

A CHOICE OF CLASSICS

Evelina Frances Burney

Subtitled *The History of a Young Lady's Entrance into the World*, the novel records in letters its young heroine's encounters with society, both high and low, in London and at fashionable watering places. It is acutely observant of the social laws regarding power, authority and authorship, which the author herself partly had to subvert.

The Republic Plato

The best-known of Plato's dialogues, *The Republic* is also one of the supreme masterpieces of Western philosophy, whose influence cannot be overestimated.

Brigitta and Other Tales Adalbert Stifter

Each of these four stories is set in a recognizable world depicted with measured realism. But once the reader has learned to look beneath the calm, apparently seamless surface of the narrative, and, in Stifter's words, 'to see with the heart', strange tensions are revealed.

The Poems of Exile Ovid

Exiled from Rome for his scandalous erotic verse and a mysterious (probably political) misdemeanour, Ovid spent his declining years in the remote Black Sea port of Tunis, trying to use poetry to win a reprieve.

The Birth of Tragedy Friedrich Nietzsche

Dedicated to Richard Wagner, *The Birth of Tragedy* created a furore on its first publication in 1871; it has since become one of the seminal books of European culture.

Madame Bovary Gustave Flaubert

With *Madame Bovary* Flaubert established the realistic novel in France while his central character of Emma Bovary, the bored wife of a provincial doctor, remains one of the great creations of modern literature.